RING OF GYGES

THE MISADVENTURES OF LOREN BOOK 2

INES JOHNSON

THOSE JOHNSON GIRLS

1

It's a universal truth that all women pretend is a myth; most men are duds. The honest truth is, there's only a handful of good ones out there. We all know it. The fairytale is believing we somehow, some way might be wrong.

But we're not.

It's not men's fault. They all come into the world with so much potential. That's because most men start their lives inside of and then attached to a woman. But inevitably, they all stray away from their mother's apron strings and meet another male.

This other male winds up introducing the mama's boy to a stream of dribble. That vitriol cleanses any common sense from the good little boy's brain. Unfortunately, oftentimes this purge is permanent and both young men wind up turning into douches.

"What about that one?" said Percival. "She's above a minimum level of acceptable attractiveness."

I looked around the pub. The bar area was dimly lit. The stale smell of the tap mixed with the musky cloud of cigarettes. A splash of antiseptic hung in the air, but my boots still stuck to the floor as I tapped my toe to a Top 40's tune. We were on the outskirts of Caerleon, away from the enchanted Tintagel castle where the magical realm of Camelot dwelled.

I sat at a table with four of the Round Table's finest. Gawain nursed a mug of frothy beer, his eyes were shuttered half-moons as they took in the crowded bar searching for Percy's pick. Tristan toyed with the long neck bottle of a craft beer as his Icelandic blue eyes searched out the target. Geraint, who'd drawn the short straw of designated driver, looked down, adding a dollop of cream to his coffee turning the liquid to the same shade as his skin.

Since I was an official knight now, I was included in the little excursion of guys' night out. Or I may have simply followed them out of the castle. Whatever.

"She's pretty but not too trendy," Percy continued after he tossed back his fourth shot of whiskey. The brown liquid did nothing to burn out his throaty Middle Eastern accent, which made his P's sound like B's. "So, she's not high maintenance. But enough fashion sense to show she cares about her appearance."

I took a healthy gulp of my rum so that my mouth was occupied. Not that anyone was asking my opinion. I took another look at the damsel these knights were about to sweep off her feet.

The woman sat alone at the end of the bar, twiddling a lock of her hair. The chair next to her was empty. She didn't have a book or a phone out, meaning she was open for approach. I could tell a lot of male eyes were on her, assessing. Likely in the same manner as the men at my table. I was getting to hear what they really thought before they went out hunting for a piece of tail.

"Her toenails are done, so good hygiene. She's wearing heels, so not a tomboy which means sex is on the table and none of that palling around, platonic friend nonsense."

The thing was, I knew Percy wasn't being mean. He was making a calculated, logical, detailed statement. What I'd learned about the knight in the last few weeks was that he had no filter. Like, none. He always said exactly what came into his disgusting male mind. Things most men wouldn't say with a woman present. But I'm sure the other knights around the table were thinking it as they looked at the women in the bar.

"She's got a good hip to waist ratio, so she can take a good sized cock. Got her hand on her hips which means she's open for business. Nice, long hair to wrap your fist around." Percy made a hand gesture as he talked about her hips and her hair. "And a clear complexion which means she's healthy. Or, she's good with a makeup kit. I'm not the best judge there. What say you, Dame Galahad? Good genes or flawless foundation?"

I blinked a couple of times, trying to process everything he'd just said. The feminist in me was stunned into silence. But the catty chick that hung around the back of my mind took the opportunity to speak up. "Oh, that's definitely foundation. No one's pores are naturally that clear."

Percy nodded, filling his glass with another finger of whiskey. "That takes it back to her caring about her appearance. All in all, a good catch for the night. Maybe even the weekend. I say go for it."

I opened my mouth to protest for my sex. But, damn it. I couldn't think of a thing to say. Although it was douchey to bring attention to all those things,

Percy was right. Even worse, women judged men the same way.

We evaluated them on how they dressed—brand name or ratty gym clothes. We looked at their hands and not just the ring finger or the distance between the index finger and thumb. We looked at the tidiness of their nails. A guy who bit his nails to nubs? Ew. A guy whose nails were longer than mine? No, thank you.

We looked at his shoe size but also the wear and tear on his soles. We looked at his body and judged his muscle to fat ratio. I dare any woman to say her lady bits got an erection at the sight of a beer belly.

"What do I say to her?" asked Tristan, who was the chivalrous warrior the battle plans were being drawn out for.

"Don't worry," said Geraint. "I'll be your wingman."

I inwardly groaned but managed to cover my disapproval with a healthy gulp of my drink. Before douches and frat boys misappropriated the term to trick unsuspecting women into sleeping with them, wingman had an entirely different meaning. It was a combat term for the positioning of aircraft pilots. The fighter jet who flew in formation to your right or left was a support role in the air. Their role was to watch your flank and make sure you didn't crash land on the ground. The bar was much like an airfield with women blaring their headlights in an erect and upright position. Men hovered around, trying to land their equipment without crashing.

"Let me give you some guidance," said Geraint.

It was kind of admirable of Geraint, wanting to help his brother-at-arms on this carnal quest. Geraint was the head trainer of the squires, but all I'd ever seen him dole out was disapproval and judgment on the jousting fields. Tonight, he looked downright encouraging talking to Tristan.

"Here's the plan," said Geraint. "I'll go over to the girl and talk you up."

"A classic maneuver." Percy raised his shot glass. "A testimonial from a friend is heftier than singing your own praises."

"You think that'll work?" asked Tristan.

"Definitely," said Geraint.

"Absolutely not," I said at the same time.

Percy gave the thumbs up.

Gawain kept his mouth shut and shook his head at his half-empty glass.

Geraint clapped Tristan on the back. The blond knight with the cherubic face took a deep breath and nodded at his brother at arms. Before they left,

Geraint rolled his eyes at me. Then he turned and corralled Tristan over to a few chairs down the bar.

I turned my attention to Gawain. "So, this is what guys' night out is like? Actually, knights' night out."

"We're just unwinding from work." Gawain picked up a greasy, battered piece of fish and then let it fall back into the basket with a soggy plop. "I told you it wouldn't be interesting."

Anything was more interesting than the last week at Camelot. The entire town had been involved in a neighborhood-wide cleanup mission after the invasion of druid priestesses intent on taking away every witch and wizard's magic. Most of the damage had been done around the moat when a sea creature rose from the waters. With its tentacles, it captured the two Queen B druidesses and took them down into the deep. Finally, everything was back in order, and we had a rare night off to kick back and relax.

Unfortunately, down at the end of the bar, I saw a plane wreck about to happen as Geraint flew off course.

"Young Tristan here graduated at the top of my class," Geraint was saying.

"So," drawled the woman, her body curved away from the blond knight and towards the dark knight, "you're a professor?"

Geraint's eyebrows rose with carnal interest. Then immediately lowered as he caught sight of his expectant brother. "No," he corrected. "I mean, I was his instructor. Just not at a university. See Tristan here—"

"What do you teach?" the woman asked, running her forefinger over her lip as she smiled up at Geraint.

Geraint's pupils tracked the motion. A bright fire ignited in his dark eyes. "Uh, battle tactics."

The knight's chest puffed up at the appreciation in the woman's gaze. But then he shook himself and turned back to Tristan. He placed a hand on the young man's arm as though presenting him like a prize.

"Tristan here, is an excellent marksman."

"Really," said the woman, gaze zeroed in on Geraint. "You are such a good friend. Can I buy you a drink?"

Geraint's pointy brows rose. His hand left Tristan's shoulder, and he turned to face the woman, shutting Tristan out. But Tristan was already trudging back to our table.

"I told you it wouldn't work," I said when Tristan slumped down in his seat.

"That's because he singled one out," said Percy.

"You have to approach women in packs, and then cull one off from the herd. It's what I like to call—"

"Percy," warned Gawain.

Percy ignored his fellow knight and plowed on. "—the hottie versus ugo maneuver."

Gawain winced.

I was only mildly offended. I'd heard worse inside fraternity houses when I was in college. I hadn't been enrolled at any of the universities I frequented. I just attended every now and then for the co-ed experience.

I'd been around my fair share of douches and hipsters on campuses. No, I saw no difference between the two brand of men. Both herds could be heard saying stupid things like, 'That's what she said,' or typing in ALL CAPS, or they were so tragically hip, that they were into each new fad before it was popular. You know the type. The ones that 'liked' all their own social media posts? Yeah, that guy.

"Take those two for example." Percy pointed to two women sitting at a nearby table. "Notice the hot one and her ug—" He eyed me. "I mean, her less attractive friend."

"They both look quite lovely to me," said Tristan.

"That's because you're young. The blonde is definitely prettier. I'll occupy the ugo, and you can swoop in and gain the attention of the hot one."

As entertained as I was at the inner workings of the male mind, I felt I should speak up. Tristan was still young enough to be saved from the unhygienic cleansing of douchery. But Percy was already pulling him up and out of the chair.

I didn't blame Tristan for trying. I knew that sex was the cure for a lot of ailments; depression, obesity, hangovers, heart disease, tooth decay, the common cold, writer's block. I knew firsthand the best use of sexual encounters was for getting over an ex-lover by climbing on top of the next one.

After my last relationship ended, I was aiming to find a new male mattress to bounce up and down on. I eyed Gawain, but I knew better. He'd already sat me down and strapped me securely into the friend zone. It had taken a few days, but we'd slipped into platonic mode. Still, I got tripped up every now and then when I looked at his high cheekbones and that strong chin. The angle of his chin was sharp enough to leave thigh burn.

"He's going to crash and burn," I said to Gawain.

"Yeah," Gawain grinned.

"You don't think we should intervene?"

"Why are you trying to stop the night's entertainment?"

"Why aren't you out there to get a warm pair of breasts for the night for yourself?" I asked him.

"Not in the mood."

Good to know I wasn't the only woman Gawain denied. He'd backed off all women. He'd told me that he had a date with death. Some while ago, Wain had faced off against a mysterious foe who he affectionately called Death. All Wain would say was that the fight wasn't finished, and he'd either emerge victorious, or dead, at the appropriately appointed time, which I supposed meant that his womanizing days were over. I wasn't sure if it was because he was trying to repent. I honestly still wasn't sure if I believed him about this future morbid date.

At the other table, Percy had snagged the ugo's attention. But the hottie was fixated on him as well. Both women aimed their headlights in the direction of his cockpit hoping to be invited into the captain's quarters. A moment later, Tristan came trudging back to our table.

"It didn't work," Tristan said.

"I told you," I said.

"You're a woman," he said. "How do I pick up girls?"

I opened my mouth, but Gawain stepped in. "She'll tell you you need to be vulnerable. That girls will look past your looks and see your manners."

I shook my head. "No, that's not something I'd ever say. You need to show confidence. Take charge of the situation. Women want Superman and his balls of steel, not Clark Kent and his four eyes. Show your bravado. Pound your chest."

"Really?" said Gawain.

"That can't be right," said Tristan.

"Excuse me? Who is the one at the table with breasts?" I said. "They come home with me every night, you know. I know what I'm talking about. See that girl?"

I pointed to an unassuming, age-appropriate, modestly dressed girl sitting alone at a table. She was looking off at the dance floor at a group that was dancing. She was probably out for a girls' night and her friend had ditched her when she got asked to dance.

"Go over there, and swagger when you walk. Lock eyes with her from a distance. But first, unbutton the top two buttons of your shirt. And here, take your hair out of that tie."

With his shirt open and his yellow locks flowing and his blue eyes wide, he looked like a young Fabio.

"So, what do I say when I get over there?" he asked.

"Actually, you don't need to say much. Just start with a smile and a hello. She'll take it from there."

Tristan got up and went over to the girl. His swagger was more of a glide. His eye lock made her fidget. But then he came into the light. That's when her eyes widened at the fine specimen that approached her, and she uncrossed and then re-crossed her legs—the true universal sign for *Come on over, baby. I'm open for business.*

"I would've expected you to be equal opportunity," said Gawain as he watched the show. "You know, compliment her brains and not her breasts."

I snorted as I watched Tristan take a seat at the woman's table. "Women are far superior to men. The only way you'll split our thighs is if we can somehow pretend you're smarter than us for a few hours."

It looked like my advice was working. The girl was chatting up Tristan. She leaned in. He let her do most of the talking. It looked like she was eating out of his hands. There might be some hope for Tristan to remain high and dry and not morph into a cleansing product.

But then the girl's glance slipped past Tristan for a second. My eyes, along with just about every woman in the bars eyes, snapped to the entryway. Two dark figures crossed the threshold of the establishment. In the door walked Arthur and Lance. All women's eyes went to them as they swaggered in. But neither Arthur nor Lance aimed to catch a single eye.

"Can I buy you a drink?" One woman came up and asked Lance.

"Thank you, but I'm not staying long."

"Can I come with you when you go?" she tried.

Lance blinked. "Thank you." He paused, likely looking for a nice way to let her down. "But, no."

He side-stepped the woman. He and Arthur took the seats vacated by the others and sat. They each slumped down as though they'd both been holding up half the world on each of their shoulders.

"What took you two so long?" asked Gawain.

"Morgan," growled Arthur.

"Merlin," growled Lance. He turned back to Arthur. "You realize he's back there alone with ... everyone."

I knew that *everyone* was code for Gwin. Anytime Lance spoke in code, it had something to do with Gwin. But no one said anything.

"The squires are there," said Arthur. "So's the old guard. Merlin can't get out of the bed. He's dying."

The look on Lance's face said *not soon enough*. But he didn't dare say those words out loud about his leader's brother. Instead, he rose from his seat. "Still, I think I should-"

Arthur reached out and handed Lance back in his chair. "Have a drink. That's an order."

Lance grumbled, but he put his hand up for the barmaid. She sauntered over, breasts first. Lance placed his order, barely glancing at the woman.

I turned to Arthur, only half curious to know what Morgan had done to itch that hard-to-reach-spot at the center of his back. But I had a more pressing query. "Any word on Baros?"

"Loren, we don't talk Table business outside of the castle." Arthur took the drink from the barmaid, caressing the glass like the body of a lover. He didn't eye the buxom beauty that had delivered the drink.

Man, half of these virile knights weren't trying to get any action. I was decidedly raring to be let off the bench. I needed some action, and badly. Problem was, I only wanted one man.

Baros was my ex. Not just any ex, The Ex. The one you never quite get over and keep getting under.

But I was done getting under him. I wanted to get on top of him. To pummel him into the ground for what he'd done to me. So, Artie may not be ready to talk about it, but I was going to find Baros and, when I did, it would be on.

Before I could figure out another way to broach the subject, Arthur's cell phone rang. It was so strange to see the device in the hands of a medieval warrior, but that was the way of this place and these people. A mix of modern and medieval.

Arthur's eyes grew large. "She did what?"

The entire bar came to a standstill at the sound of his roar. He shot up and made a signal. All the knights fell in formation. I was a bit late to get up and in line. I didn't know that particular signal. It hadn't come in the memo along with the secret handshake for knights.

"What is it?" asked Gawain once we were outside and out of earshot of the humans.

"The castle kitchen is on fire," growled Arthur.

"Are we under attack?" said Geraint.

"It's Merlin, isn't it?" asked Lance.

"No," said Arthur. "It's Morgan."

2

———

"I had it under control."

Morgan was covered in soot. Her hands were cocked on her hips, and her features were clear with indignation as she glared at Arthur. There were burn marks on the ceiling of the kitchen. A rancid smell of chemicals and spoiled food filled the air. The glass window had a hairline crack that wasn't receding. It was growing.

"Control is what you need, all right," growled Arthur. "You need to be put on a leash to control you."

"Try it, and I will bite you."

The two faced off against one another. Tension was thick in the room as their chests heaved.

"It's all right," came Gwin's soothing voice. She stepped between her lord and her sister, ever the peacemaker. "No extensive damage has been done. We can have this cleaned up by the morning."

"With no help from her," said Arthur. But then he jerked back in immediate shame.

Morgan's chin steeled. "That's right. Blame it on the impotent witch."

"I didn't mean ..." But Arthur's voice trailed off. He would no longer meet Morgan's gaze. That was a tactical mistake on his part. Morgan didn't like pity.

"My hands still work even if my magic is gone. I'll clean up my own mess," she said.

"I'll help," I said. After all, it was my fault that Morgan had lost her powers.

Before the Banduri priestesses brought their battle to the castle, they'd surrounded Morgan and me at the top of the Tor in Glastonbury. Morgan had been cut by the Spear of Destiny. When the blade broke her skin, it leeched out her powers. The only reason Morgan had been there was because she'd followed me.

"So will I," said Gwin. "We'll take care of this."

Arthur looked around the room at the show of solidarity between the Galahad girls. That's what we called ourselves. The three of us were the last descendants of Sir Galahad. One of us, Arthur might argue with and win. But all three of us? He was a smart leader. He backed down.

He turned to Morgan. "Let this be the last time you play at chemistry in the kitchen."

"This wasn't play," said Morgan. "I'm a scientist. I was working on my craft. And if I had my own lab and equipment this wouldn't have happened."

"We've already been through this, Morgan. We're not building a lab in the castle."

"Then I'll go away to school. That's what mortals do."

Arthur's jaw steeled. "It's not safe. And you're not mortal."

"I'm not a witch, so there's no threat to me."

"Without your powers, you can't protect yourself." He turned on his heel.

"You wouldn't let me go when I had powers and now that I don't you still won't. You can't have it both ways."

But Arthur had already exited the kitchen, and the knights filed out after him.

"Are you really going to marry him?" Morgan turned on her sister as the men left the room.

Lance was the last out. I saw his back stiffen at Morgan's muttered retort.

"Nothing's been decided," said Gwin. But she said it to a retreating Lance who walked stiff as a board. Gwin gazed after him until the door swung shut. Then she sighed and began a spell. She twiddled her fingers and then made a come-hither motion. A bucket rose into the air and began filling itself with water. "Besides, Arthur hasn't asked. It's a moot point since I'm still married."

"To a homicidal maniac," I said.

I started my own spell, mimicking Gwin's finger motions. My bucket rose into the air. And then emptied out the dirty water in its belly.

Gwin smiled encouragingly at me. I was getting better and better with my magic, but there were still kinks to work out. Instead of mopping with clean water, I called a small army of sponges to deal with my mess.

"I'm not disputing Merlin's character flaws," said Gwin. "But he's dying. And until he's gone, my vows remain intact. You know, in sickness and health."

Gwin's husband Merlin was thought dead for decades. But he resurfaced a couple of months ago when we learned he'd been siphoning off witches' powers to keep himself alive. He'd brought the fight home to Camelot, but we defeated him. Actually, I did. But I'm not one to brag.

After all the death and destruction Merlin had caused, he was resting comfortably in the infirmary upstairs. The people of Camelot had enough tolerance and compassion to hear out Judas over supper. It was both awe-inspiring and maddening.

"You're not trying to heal him, are you?" I asked. I rung out one of the sponges with a squeeze of my fist and sent it back into battle with the floor.

Gwin shook her head, waving her hand to repair the crack in the glass window. "Nothing can heal him. It's only a matter of time before he passes on."

"And then you'll marry Arthur and take your place as the Lady of Camelot?" Morgan's tone was one of strained nonchalance. She leaned her chin on the rounded handle of a broom. Dust bunnies gathered at her boots.

Gwin didn't notice her sister's tone or inaction. Her gaze was fixed on the door where the knights had exited. I know her mind was focused on one knight in particular, and that knight was not Arthur. But neither Gwin nor Lance would admit their feelings for one another.

Camelot was nothing, if not a soap opera. There were television sets and computers with internet all over the castle. But I hadn't caught up on TGIT, Thank God It's Thursday, television since I came here. Nothing could surpass the drama of this place.

"Is the fascist letting you go on the mission to find your ex-boyfriend?" asked Morgan, turning the attention back to my dramatic love life.

"Baros wasn't my boyfriend."

It was an automatic response, followed by me looking around worried that he may have heard someone say it. The term was decidedly American and from a long-dead era. I firmly believed that no one over the age of sixteen should ever be caught using it.

Even when I was a teen, it felt a bit infantilizing. Shy glances, awkward fumblings, stolen kisses? Nope. Those had never been my thing. I was not shy or awkward about my sexuality.

"Significant other?" tried Gwin.

I grimaced. Other than my dad, all the significant people in my life had been women. Men came and went.

True, Baros and I had made the rounds on each other a number of times in the past. And, yes, many of the significant events in my life had happened with him in the vicinity. But putting those two words together *significant* and *other* and then pointing them at Baros felt off.

Morgan put the broom aside and took a seat on the counter. "What was your relationship with him then?"

Even the R-word made me cringe. There was such a permanence to it. It made my neck get hot.

"He was my lover," I answered. "A friend with benefits. A bed buddy."

"So, it was just sex?" Morgan nodded appreciatively.

Gwin frowned at me with a headshake I knew meant 'don't encourage her.'

"Sex and swords," I amended.

Baros had been my sword master when my father had been working on the Parthenon restorations in Greece. I'd become a formidable swordswoman by the age of twelve. Baros was the best swordsmen I'd ever encountered. I later found out that was because he was a Spartan warrior, The Spartan warrior, actually.

Leonidas was once the famed king of Sparta, the one who led the 300 into their ill-fated battle against Xerxes's Persian army. He'd supposedly died in that battle. But the Greek god, Zeus, had chosen him as he lay dying on the battlefield and made him an immortal servant of the Olympians.

Lenny had been reborn, but his hatred of Persians survived the rebirth. He'd secretly waged war against the nation and its culture for centuries until his last battle in Eleusis, Greece. He'd sided with the Titans which nearly broke the world and sent Lenny on the run.

"Why would you want to go after him?" asked Gwin. "He's hurt you more than once already."

"Hurt"—the four-lettered emotion landed heavy on my tongue—"is a big word."

"You never get over your first love," said Gwin.

"Love," I choked. "There was no love. I'm not you, Gwin, I don't believe in that fairytale nonsense."

On the grounds of Camelot, inside the four walls of the castle's kitchen, trash magically made its way into the garbage. Birds chirped outside, but none of them came into the repaired window to help.

"Why not?" asked Gwin. "Every little girl deserves a fairytale."

"Yeah, but we're not little girls," said Morgan.

"That's right," I said. "We're Galahad girls."

"True," said Gwin. "But if anyone deserves a fairytale, it's certainly us."

Each one of us opened our mouths to agree. But the monosyllabic agreement we were about to utter died on our lips. We were Galahad girls. We should've been prime candidates for princes. Hell, we lived with a bunch of knights from the storybooks.

But, here you had, Morgan, a hundred fifty-year-old virgin who'd never been on a date. There was Gwin, who turned out to marry the villain in the story. And then there was me, an ardent commitment-phobe who choked every time she tried to say the R-word out loud.

"You know what we need ladies?" I walked over to the fridge. "Midnight margaritas."

"It's not midnight," said Morgan.

"I've never had a margarita," said Gwin.

"We're three witches, lamenting about our love lives, in a kitchen," I said. "This totally calls for a dancing montage with spirits."

"I'm not a witch," said Morgan.

"You're currently a non-practicing witch," I said, "which means you qualify. But even better, you are the best chemist in Camelot."

With a flick of my wrist, I shoved the sponges off to the side and went to the cupboards to pull out the ingredients. "We'll need the juice of a green lizard.

Also, a handful of white sand from the loch of a sea monster."

Morgan giggled as I handed her the lime and salt.

"Gwin, grab me the cold crystals while I go and get the most important ingredient in this spell from the potions cabinet."

Gwin headed to the icebox while I dug around in the liquor cabinet. I immediately found the tequila. I saw a bottle of orange spirits with a label I couldn't read and figured what the hell.

"Everything goes into the cauldron," I said plugging in the blender. "Now flip the switch and let the cauldron bubble."

Our giggles mixed with the motor of the blender and the crunching of the ice and the slushing of the alcohol. But that was nothing to when we each took our first sip of the concoction.

I pointed my finger at a radio in the corner of the kitchen and it began playing music. The three of us started a conga line. We twirled around, waving our arms and swaying our hips to the beat. Morgan took center stage doing a body wave that ended with a hair flip. Then Gwin surprised me, wiggling her hips to the beat and shimmying her shoulders. By the time we got around to my turn, the jig was up.

"Girls!" came a growling Celtic voice. "What's going on in there?"

"Nothing," we singsonged and then cackled with laughter as we topped off our glasses.

Gwin managed to turn and lock the door before Arthur or any of the knights could make their way in. This party did not include them. It was girls' night now.

3

"Ready. Charge."

Geraint's booming voice sounded over the heaving breaths and heavy boots. The jousting area had been transformed into a blank green and muddy slate. The horses were stabled, and gone were the wooden rail barriers of the tilt. The lances were put away and the quintain targets were shoved off to the side. Out on the training ground of Tintagel Castle, the field was open for all-out warfare. With me at the head of the pack, all the squires charged each other with a battle cry.

Yes, even though I had been knighted a couple of weeks ago, I was still required to undertake the trials. Something or other about tradition and preparedness. I don't know? I wasn't paying attention when Geraint spoke. I rarely did.

To most of the women of Camelot, Geraint's voice was silky and smooth as words rolled off his tongue with a hint of his North African accent. But to me? His voice tended to grate on my nerves.

However, this new chapter of squire training was actually fun. We were training for what to do in a large battle. I suppose?

The squires had been broken into two teams. After quarreling over who were the good guys (my team) and who were the bad guys (the other team), we took our places on opposite sides of the field. When Geraint's grating voice gave the command, we rammed into each other with vicious glee. It was so much fun!

We were all armed with swords, and we still wore chainmail over our chests. The steel of the mail was enchanted. The magic easily protected us from the practice swords and shields we used, and it with-stood many other magical assaults. But witches and knights did have a weakness as I'd learned in the last battle fought on this very field.

Bluestones were our own form of kryptonite. The Banduri had brought nearly a ton of the stuff with them during their invasion. As we'd fought the

Banduri only a couple of weeks ago, small rocks, pebbles, and dust of the foul stones had seeped into the ground. But with some elbow grease and a lot of magic, the townsfolk had raked all the hazardous debris from the grounds just in time for training to resume.

At first glance, the training exercise looked like a free for all. But there was actually some order to the chaotic melee. It was basically capture the flag. But the trick was that we all had a sword in one hand and a shield in the other. If you dropped either of your weapons, by force or by happenstance, you were out.

I spotted my buddy, Maurice, who had gotten swiped up by the other team. I gave him a sorry-not-sorry grimace. His amiable grin morphed into a challenging smirk. Then it was on.

I charged the mountain of a young man. All six-foot tall and one-hundred-twenty pounds of me crashed into the nearly seven-foot tall and two-hundred-fifty pounds of him. He barely budged. Meanwhile, I felt my teeth rattle in my tonsils.

Maurice looked like a teddy bear, but he was made like that metal X-man—what was his name? Anyway, the colossal giant before me brandished his sword and attacked. I parried with my shield and was able to protect myself, but again, it didn't budge him.

"You lot need to get used to fighting one-handed," said Percy. "Stop using the shield as a counterbalance. It's a weapon of defense. Not a weight."

Both Maurice and I brought our swords and shields up. Maurice stood squarely in front of me. I stood in more of a side lunge stance, due to my fencing training. I never gave anyone full frontal access, no matter what any man might have said about me.

The square stance made no sense to me. I knew that the edge of the shield was weaker than the center. And so I simply struck the edge, which opened up Maurice's body. As predicted, his forearm followed his shield and he lost his grip. His shield fell to the ground, and without my having to go through his big bear of a body, he was out of the game and out of my way.

I gripped my shield tight to my body and turned to find my next opponent. Boys were falling on both sides, mainly due to the weakness of their shield technique. Instead of attacking the body, they were all attacking the edge of the shields and trying to force their opponents to lose their grips.

It was working. It was also boring. I failed to see

the point of the exercise, so I directed my attention elsewhere. And there it was.

The flag was in sight. In fact, my teammate, Yuric, was upon it. But he froze as he tried to determine how to pick it up without setting down either his sword or his shield. His hesitation cost him. Baysle, the perpetual leader of the other guys, took a swing at him.

It was unnecessary roughness as Baysle disarmed Yuric by tapping at the edge of his shield. The villain then went further and took the blunt end of his sword and shoved it into Yuric's gut. The chainmail protected us from any mortal slicing that would rend our flesh, but it didn't do much to soften the impact of blows.

Yuric went down gasping for air, and leaving Baysle free to take the flag and the victory for the opposing team. Unfortunately for Baysle, he was then confronted with the exact same conundrum as Yuric. How the hell would he take possession of the flag without putting down either of his weapons which would automatically expel him from the game? Even worse for Baysle, the fight wasn't over. I was his next opponent.

Baysle's upper lip curled when he saw me standing, backlit by the sun. A light wind blew the tendrils of my hair out of my face. I heard crickets chirping in the blades of grass, a bird cawing from a tree. I did that slow advance like you see in movies before the climactic fight scene. A branch cracked under Baysle's foot as he made an equally slow advance on me. Then we squared off, facing each other.

"So," I drawled in an awful Spanish accent, "now it is down to you, and it is down to me."

Baysle brought his shield to his chest and lifted his sword.

"Hello," I tilted my head. "My name is Loren Van Alst. You kill my friend. Prepare to die."

Baysle looked behind him at our fallen comrades. "What is she even talking about?"

I sighed. "You kids need to watch more eighties movies."

Instead of playing along with the storybook romance of princesses, pirates, and vengeful Spaniards, Baysle charged me. I lunged forward, striking the edge of his shield. No one was more surprised than me when he shifted his body, and my blade glanced off his disk. The kid had actually learned from past mistakes. Who knew?

But now I had to smarten up too. Baysle's shield came back at me, the edge aimed at my face like it was a blade. I bent my body backward, Matrix-style, and then struck out with my foot. Baysle went down, but he didn't lose his grip on his weaponry. He managed a cool martial arts move which landed him back on his feet without the use of his hands.

Okay. So, he was actually going to make me break a sweat? The little creep.

We came at each other again. This time, taking a tactic from Baysle's cookbook, I used my shield like a sword. Aiming for his shield hand, I went for the edge of his shield with mine. The move pushed both of our shields into the armpit of his sword hand, leaving him entirely defenseless. His whole body was open to my attack.

I aimed my sword for his jewels. "Yield."

Baysle grit his teeth. His green eyes screamed bloody murder.

Oh, it would get bloody all right. If he didn't drop his weapons, I was going to relieve him of a couple of his toys. But the boy was smart. He threw his sword down to the ground in a huff. Then he backed away from me, dropping his shield down low to protect what he prized most in his life.

There was no one left standing on the battlefield. Look at that. I'd won.

But there was no cheering just yet. Now, I was

confronted with the exact same problem that had stumped both Yuric and Baysle. How to pick up the flag without setting down either of my weapons?

I kicked at the flag's staff, which was speared deeply into the ground. It didn't budge.

I squatted down over it and tried to grab it between my knees and toppled over. I heard chuckling behind me.

"Oh, shut up," I said. "Not one of you got this far."

I saw Geraint and Percy eyeing me from the sidelines. Percy looked maniacally amused. Geraint looked bored and constipated.

I turned back to the flag. There was no way a normal person without a third hand could pick this dang thing up. And then I remembered. I wasn't normal. I was a witch.

But my hands were full. I couldn't flick my fingers like I'd done with the bucket and mop last night. I decided the thing to do was to pull a Samantha.

I wiggled my nose bewitchingly. The flag blew on a nonexistent breeze, but it didn't come up. I wiggled my nose again. The earth around the staff began to give way. I wiggled it a third time, and the flag flew up and balanced on the tip of my sword.

Geraint's pointy eyebrows flattened. Percy's grin rose higher. The bad guys moaned and booed at my display of magic. The good guys cheered me on for the win.

"You missed the whole point of the exercise." Geraint marched over to me, his fists balled at his sides.

"Uh, the point was to win," I said. "And I did. There was no rule that said I couldn't use magic."

"No," said Geraint. "The point is to never put down your weapon. That's the lesson in all of this. When you're on the battlefield, no prize is worth your life."

"Oooh," I nodded, pondering the moral of the story. "That's pretty deep. And I totally get your point."

"Actually, G," said Percy. "I think she makes another point."

Percy came up and studied me. Under the scrutiny of his dark gaze, I began to squirm. Sir Percival was rumored to have been raised in the wild. Looking in his predatory gaze was like having a dark light flashing directly into my eyes. It made no sense for darkness to be bright, but that's what it felt like to me. His lips were spread wide like a wolf's, ready to sink sharp incisors into my flesh.

"We have a witch in our midst," Percy proclaimed.

"Yeah," I nodded, wondering if he were playing with a full deck. Wondering also if it was smart that he be let near children.

"She's a witch and a warrior," Percy continued as though he hadn't heard me. "Don't you see, G? We can use her like a weapon. If she can pick up a stick without hands, she can probably throw a punch from a distance."

"You know," I said, latching onto his manic enthusiasm. "I had this idea. You ever watch *Star Trek*."

Percy looked quizzically at me. I forgot; raised in the wild. I turned to the squires.

"Dr. Spock? Captain Kirk?"

The squires nodded. So, they'd watched seventies television but skipped the eighties movies.

"I loved Zachary Quinto the first couple of seasons in *Heroes*," said Yuric. "And then it got old. But he kicked butt as Spock."

I rolled my eyes at the mention of the remake of the classic television show into a film with Millennial actors. But a girl had to work with what she had.

"You remember Spock's Vulcan nerve pinch?" I spread my fingers into the V of the Vulcan greeting.

"He used it to render his victims unconscious because it was supposed to be undignified for a Vulcan to knock someone out with a physical punch."

"Oh, is that the reason?" said Maurice.

"Spock touches a pressure point at the base of the neck using telepathic energy from his fingertips," I said. "Since magic is a bunch of energy, what if I could send a bunch of energy to that bunch of nerves from a distance?"

Geraint opened his mouth to protest. Before he could get in a word, Percy stepped in front of him. Percy rubbed his bearded chin as he stared at me again with those dark, bloodthirsty eyes.

"Let's try it," Percy said with a sly grin.

"Percy," growled Geraint in warning.

Percy wrapped an arm around Geraint's shoulders. The move was probably meant to be brotherly, but it looked as though Percy was holding his brother-at-arms at bay. "What if she could incapacitate a whole army with a flick of her wrist? Less work for us."

In the end, Geraint threw up his hands. Percy gave me the thumbs up. I turned to the squires.

"Any volunteers?" I asked.

The boys looked around at each other. Feet shuffled and kicked up dirt. Hands fidgeted on sword handles and tugged at chainmail. Finally, Maurice stepped forward.

His amiable grin was back in place after the battle, letting me know we were back on the same side again. I gave him a smile right back, hoping that after this display we would still be friends. I was far more sure of my fighting skills than I was of my magic skills. But what I was about to do was magical fighting. So, it should work. Right?

I took a deep, cleansing breath. All that managed to do was to awaken the butterflies in my belly. I blinked a couple of times and focused my attention. But trying to quiet my mind had never worked. I heard everything.

Baysle's breathing. Geraint's eyebrows twitching. Percy grinding his incisors.

I decided to try a chant. "Bring me quiet, bring me peace. Bring this big man to his knees."

The energy swirled between my V-spread fingers. I threw out my hand towards Maurice. And ... nothing happened.

I tried again. Another deep cleansing breath. Another few blinks of the eyes. I even tossed in a head waggle, hoping to clear my mind. I spread my fingers into a Vulcan V again.

"Engineering is red. Science is blue. With this V, I conquer you."

This time when I aimed my peaceful greeting at Maurice he shrugged his right shoulder up. Then he jerked it up to his ear, as though someone was pinching him. Then he shrugged his left shoulder. His chest began to shake. His hands swatted at his neck as though a bug buzzed around him. He swatted more frantically as if a horde of bugs had descended on him.

Next, the big guy fell to the ground. At first, I was afraid he was in pain, and I'd pinched a nerve that might leave damage. But then the giggles started. As big as he was, Maurice let out a trill of giggles fit for an afternoon tea party with kindergarten girls. Everyone looked up at me as he rolled from side to side on the ground trying to shake off my spell.

"Okay," I said. "Maybe I need a bit more practice."

All the boys backed up at least three paces. So, I might not have hit the right nerve. But my target was incapacitated and that was the goal. It didn't look like it would leave any permanent damage. At least, I hoped not.

4

—————

"I'm really sorry about that, big guy," I said.

Maurice's body had shaken for a quarter hour until someone went to get Gwin to come out and stop the spell. During that time, Maurice had giggled a high pitch squeal like a little girl while his body convulsed uncontrollably. Anything I'd tried to do only made it worse.

"You didn't do it on purpose, Lady Lo," he said.

I reached out to touch Maurice, and he jerked away from me. He smiled apologetically and headed on down the hall.

I looked down at my hands. They were already lethal with a blade. Now they could fell a man with a snap. They were empty now but I felt the energy in the air.

I hadn't hurt Maurice on purpose. But I could have. I had no business wielding my powers on living creatures when I still struggled with my control over inanimate objects. I could've done serious damage to the kid, maybe even permanent damage. I needed to keep my hands and my magic to myself until I had better control.

"You could've done serious damage to Maurice. Maybe even permanent damage."

I turned to face the sound of Geraint's voice. The hair at the back of my neck stood at the disapproving grumble of his voice. My arms crossed over my chest in a defensive pose.

"Maurice is fine," I insisted. "He got to show his feminine, softer side with all that giggling. Girls dig a man who's in touch with his femininity."

"You need to keep your hands and your magic to yourself until you have better control."

I knew he was right. I'd come to the same conclusion only five seconds ago. But now that it was coming through his pie hole, it sounded like a record scratching.

"Why are you coming down on me? It was Percy's idea."

"Yeah, well Percival can be a loose cannon. You two have that in common."

"It all worked out in the end."

"Only because of Gwin; a witch who's trained and knows what she's doing."

"You know," I said. "I thought we were cool after the battle with the Banduri."

"We're coworkers," he corrected. "But you're not one of my brothers."

"That's not something I can ever be, dude, or did you fail sex education? I'm following the rules. I'm not stepping out of line or flying solo. What more do you want from me?"

Geraint studied me. "I want to be able to trust you. To not question your every move and motive."

"So, put on a blindfold and fall back in my arms. I'll catch you." Probably.

He shook his head. "I'm not there yet."

"Isn't that your problem and not mine?"

He only glared.

I spread my arms wide. "I'm an open book."

As Geraint continued to stare, I crossed my arms over my chest. His dark gaze didn't make me feel as though he'd eat me like Percy's did. Geraint's glare felt like it saw through the bullshit.

"Tell me about Baros," he said.

I lifted my chin with a confidence I didn't feel and hoped his BS meter was off today. "What do you want to know?"

"Whatever you think is important to help your fellow knights find this magical Ring of Gyges."

The thing about BSing and confidence games? They worked best when the mark asked a specific question. But an open-ended one like that? I fixed my features so that I wasn't scowling at Geraint and searched for something to give him. But the truth was that I had nothing left to give.

Wow. Wasn't that the story of my relationship with Leonidas Baros. Though relationship is a loaded word. Baros and I had had a wide and varied connection ... association ... involvement.

We'd been student and teacher. We'd been friends and lovers. We'd been partners and then, somehow, we'd wound up on opposing teams.

This actually wasn't the first time Lenny and I had found ourselves on opposing fields. In our romantic relationship, we were often after different things. Where I was after his attention, he was always doling it out to other women besides me.

Lenny and I had had an open relationship. It wasn't like he'd duped me into it. I didn't believe in monogamy from a young age. All my life, people had been transient. No one and nothing stayed forever. Not my parents, not any of my so-called friends, or even pets I'd rescued from the streets.

As a kid, I'd traveled the world over. My family never stayed in one place for too long. I was used to making friends one day, leaving them the next day, and losing touch a month later. We'd promise to write or virtually chat and didn't. I'd return a year later, and those bosom buddies had moved on or forgotten about me completely.

My father and I had stayed in Greece the longest and returned there the most. Leonidas Baros never forgot me. We always picked up where we left off on the mat and later on the mattress. But that wasn't something the knights wanted to know.

"I didn't think so," said Geraint as my silence loomed between us.

"I don't know where he is," I insisted. "I would tell you if I did."

"Are you still in love with him?"

My nose crinkled. My feminine sensibilities had been completely offended by his words. "I was never in love with him."

Geraint stared at me. I left myself open to his radar and meters. His brows rose in surprise to see that I had told the truth.

I'd crushed on Baros hard when I was a teenager. But by the time I became a woman, I knew the score. I'd seen him juggle enough women to know that he didn't subscribe to the Highlander theory of life. For Baros, there never could be only one.

I'd figured that out for myself, but he'd reinforced it with words.

"There's no such thing as fairytales," he'd say after he'd snatched a Harlequin book from my hands when I was thirteen.

I'd been sitting on the mat waiting for my session to begin. He'd tossed the book, the pages fluttering in the air like the wings of a downed bird. Then he sliced at me with his sword. I ducked and rolled, rising to my feet to meet his next attack.

"Damsels die. Real women carry blades," he'd said when I was fifteen.

I'd been standing outside his training studio chatting up a local boy. I'd flipped my hair and giggled like I'd seen girls do in the movies. I'd pushed my weapons case behind my back when Baros had poked his head out of the door. When I came into the studio moments later, Baros said those words and advanced on me before I could unzip my weapons bag to defend myself.

"There's no such thing as a happily-ever-after.

Happiness is a constant, hard-fought battle to be won." That time, when he'd delivered his words and then his blade, I was seventeen.

It was the year my father had died. I hadn't gone back to my dad's family. I hadn't needed to. With his passing, I came into my inheritance. It was enough that I didn't need a real job until ... well, ever.

Money had never truly mattered to me. Don't get me wrong. I liked the finer things in life. Especially when it was on someone else's dime.

I liked adventure, digging for treasure, hunting for priceless artifacts, being the one to claim the find that everyone sought. The priceless treasure I sought was Leonidas Baros. After years of sitting at the kiddie table, I was done playing footsie with him. So, I emancipated myself after my dad's death and moved to Greece to be with Baros ... to train.

The age of consent was fifteen in Greece. But even as I neared my eighteenth birthday Lenny was playing hard to get. I was under no delusions that he'd fall madly in love with me and change his ways. But neither was it like I didn't believe in love. I had eyes and a library of VHS romcoms—without a working tape player, mind you. I'd witnessed the storybook love of Wesley and Buttercup, the stereophonic devotion of Lloyd to Diane. Hell, I'd seen my parents.

But also, being the observant person that I was, I knew this type of thing didn't happen to everybody. Maybe it was because I'd never had a friendship that stuck, maybe it was because I only got a few precious years with my mother, maybe it was because my father had brought me up around polygamous cultures, but somehow, I always knew that a true love story would not be for me.

Don't feel bad for me. I got my kicks in, and it all began with Lenny. Not sexually. I knew better than to offer him my virginity. I'd lost that a while ago with um ... It doesn't matter.

When I showed up on his doorstep both looking like, as well as legally, every bit a grown woman, I knew he'd struggled between turning me away and keeping me as a student. I was his prodigy. But now I was lethal with a straight blade as well as with my womanly curves.

I remembered the day it happened. We were working on a particular move; a *parry sixte avec riposte.*

"*En guarde,*" Baros called with his thick Greek accent. The lilting French words never rolled off his tongue. He crashed about the vowels like a drill sergeant might make love.

"Attack," he commanded.

I lunged into him. He held for a second until my blade was nearly upon him. Not until I extended myself, did he offer a defense.

He began with a parry. A parry was a defensive action by the one being struck. It was used to stop the blade of the opponent. It was a simple enough maneuver, just a flick of your wrist to use your blade to move theirs aside. But Baros waited until I was nearly upon him to parry.

Though the tip of the blade is the sharpest point of the sword, it's also the weakest. With my blade being so close to his wrists and the base of his sword, he parried with the forte of his sword. In contrast to the hilt, the forte at the base of the sword was the strongest part of the weapon. So, when Baros's forte met my hilt, I lost control of the fight. With just a flick of his wrist, he was able to riposte—or attack me.

We were standing nose to nose with my blade trapped and his blade angling into my breasts. So were his eyes—angling down to look at my breasts. I held still knowing he had to be the one to make the move.

But I've always been an impatient and aggressive girl. With his sword aimed at my heart, I leaned in and stole a kiss. He didn't stop me. He didn't scold me. He didn't exactly kiss me back.

When we broke apart, he raised his sword. "*En guarde.*"

I did as I was commanded. Without warning, he attacked me. I waited.

When his blade was near enough to my heart, I parried with my forte and his hilt went to his side. But when I went to riposte, he ducked out of my reach. Away from my eager blade and my hungry mouth.

"Again," he said.

This time I attacked. He waited for me, but I was ready for him. He parried.

Before he could riposte, I ducked down and out of his reach. But he'd changed the game on me again. He followed me down to the ground where another match was fought. We both let go of our swords and our hands found each other's flesh.

Long after my fighting session had ended, we came away sweaty, writhing, and sated. Clearly, I was the victor. And I had had more than one victory.

That night, I thought just maybe this could turn into a storybook love. I spent the day mooning over him. I went to my landlord and inquired about a longer lease. I went shopping for actual dinner plates instead of the paper and plastic products I bought every couple of weeks.

When I returned to his place for my next session, I got the lesson of my life. I walked in to find Baros riposting on top of another woman. Neither saw me as I backed out.

I knew he did it on purpose. It was another lesson, and I got it. This was no fairytale. I was no damsel, I carried a blade. Happiness was a battle, not a given.

I got it. It was the story of my life. But if I'm being honest, it cut deep. Other than my parents, Baros had been the only other constant in my life.

I didn't let him see me cry. I waited outside the door until he was finished. I smirked at the woman who preceded him out of the door. She looked like the only blade she ever lifted was a nail file. I knew he was toying with her, just like he'd toyed with so many others. He and I didn't play around, we fought.

I offered him a friendly greeting and came in. I took my lesson like normal. I think my nonchalance intrigued him. So, I kept it up. I let him chase me, tripping over my slow walking feet trying to get caught.

Our relationship was on again and off again for years. He never remained faithful. But whoever he was with when I came around, he always nudged her to the side to give me attention. It was something. Not quite enough. But better than nothing. And I took it.

What did I get in the end? He offered me up as a sacrifice to a Titan god. I think?

See, here's what I can't get out of my mind. I keep playing that night back in Eleusis over and over again.

I was standing before Hera, the brother-loving, daddy's girl of a goddess who was trying to raise her homicidal father from the underworld. Baros stepped into the fray. His back was to Hera; his blade was to me.

There'd been sorrow in his eyes. I think?

There'd been hesitation in his movements when Hera had commanded him to move. I think?

What I know for sure is that his wrist flicked, and his blade glinted in the moonlight as it advanced on me. But I ducked and rolled out of his reach. He didn't follow me down as he could've. He stayed standing and let me get away.

I think?

It had been a *parry sixte avec riposte*. A move we'd

practiced more times than I cared to remember both on the mat that first night and in the bedroom countless nights after. It was a move we both knew very well.

Had he expected me to evade him? Or had he actually tried to kill me? I had to know. It was the only way to get closure.

"Loren? Loren!"

I turned my attention back to Geraint. It looked as though he'd been calling my name for a while.

"Is that it?" he said.

"Is that what?" I said.

"Is that all you have to tell us about Baros?"

I nodded. "Yup. Trust me, I want to find him as much as you. I need to get some closure on the past."

5

$\mathcal{I}$ walked down the halls of Tintagel castle. The passageways were alive with the laughter of children running about. Some played childish games. Others practiced their spells.

Boys ran about with wooden swords. They were followed by some girls with pointed weapons drawn. But most girls carried around dolls and cradled poppets.

A few couples meandered arm-in-arm like something out of a Victorian promenade. Those couples probably had been born in the Victorian era and kept their etiquette and mannerisms. But it wasn't like you didn't come upon a dark corner and find some gallant man throwing his prim paramour up against a wall and kissing her senseless.

Camelot was a mix of old and new. It was a place of honor and revelry. It was home.

I made my way to the Throne room. The doors were open. I stood on the threshold for a moment, just staring in. It still gave me a thrill each time I entered this room.

The ceilings were vaulted high into the sky. The windows rose halfway toward the roof, which meant they were over twelve feet tall. Before each window was a column with flags and lances raised in salute. Iron chandeliers hung on chains with candles that held flames that were never doused. They were magical of course.

There was a subdued opulence about the place. At the center, as though it grew from roots in the ground, was the Round Table. I'd never seen the tree to make wood like that. It was a rich brown that had shades of red and orange and gold. The gnarled bark was smooth to the touch. The rings of the tree, which was used to determine the arbor's age, started at the center and ran to the edge. I'd tried counting it once and got lost before reaching the middle of the table. It was magical. I'd learned that it came from a different realm and was a gift from fairies.

I wasn't sure if the person who told me that story was telling the truth or spinning a tale. That was a common occurrence with the stories floating through these halls. They all sounded so fantastical, but they could also be the absolute truth.

Arthur and the rest of the other knights were already present. I made my way over to my family seat. I always felt like I was on a runway as I walked toward it. I swear I felt the spotlight on my back. I felt the sparkles falling from the sky. I imagined the flash of a camera and the *ahhs* of the crowd as all eyes hung on my catwalk to the chair.

"Anytime now, Dame Galahad," said Arthur.

I took my seat. As always, the cushions and backrest molded to my form, letting me know that this seat was meant for me. It was an honor I strove to prove worthy of every day of my life.

Once I was seated, Arthur ran through the day's business. It was much like a board meeting. I'd been bummed that we didn't do a ritual dance or have a sacred song that we all sang or even a secret handshake. Nope. It was all about responsibilities and duties.

"Percival," said Arthur, "your reports from the Banduri."

"They've kept to their word so far," said Percy. "Apparently they voted to be on the side of good and that includes no killing of witches and wizards. I believe we can trust the new leadership, Thalia. But there are pockets of older Banduri who still look upon us as thieves of the Garden."

Arthur shook his head, tipping it back and looking upward. The Banduri priestesses were an ancient problem he didn't want to deal with in the present. The women had tormented me back in private school, and I'd prefer not to deal with them again myself. But we couldn't choose our own villains.

Arthur turned to Gawain to inquire about another ancient foe. "What news of the Templars?"

"They've been quiet of late," said Gawain. "Which can only mean they're planning something big if history is to be our guide."

The Templars were the Knights' sworn enemies. They had once been allied, but when the Knight's Templars came under the rule of the church, the Templars turned on the Knights of Camelot. Much for the same reason as the Banduri. Both groups thought the knights and witches were in league with the devil.

It was laughable if you spent even an hour with these townsfolk. The witches, wizards, knights, and people of Camelot were a tight-knit family that only looked to keep the dangers of the supernatural world away from themselves and the rest of the world. They had no designs on rulership outside of this small town. They had no care to lead others' souls toward or away from any particular god. They were all Christians, for God's sake. Something I still struggled with.

"We'll need to strengthen the outposts," Arthur was saying.

"The new batch of squires won't be ready to take on a ley line for at least another year or two."

There were different types of knights, I'd learned. There were the Knights of the Roundtable that stayed in Camelot and protected the large population at Castle Tintagel. But there were smaller castles and magical places on the ley lines where a smaller population of witches and wizards lived. Once squires were knighted, they were often sent to these outposts to guard these people. One such place, if you can believe it, was Disneyland.

"On to other business," said Arthur. "What more do we know about Baros and the Ring of Gyges?"

My ears perked up. Finally, we were getting to what I considered the main event of these proceedings. Showtime.

It was Geraint that spoke up. "All we know is

what the ring does. It allows the wearer to become invisible."

"Or possibly invincible," said Lance.

"The translation is poor," agreed Arthur. "Do we know if the ring is fae?"

"Possibly," shrugged Geraint. "There are stories of such a ring throughout the history books, but not much about Gyges. It's not clear if he was a shepherd or a king or even a real man. The story was written by Plato."

"Oh!" I raised my hand like I was in grade school. All the knights turned and raised quizzical brows at me.

"You don't have to raise your hand to speak, my lady," said Arthur. "If you have something to add, wait your turn and then speak."

I lowered my hand. "Is it my turn?" I addressed this to Geraint.

He rolled his eyes. "No, I wasn't finished."

I glared at him and pursed my lips. But the pinched expression on my face slipped as the chair cushions coddled and caressed my shoulders and back.

"Plato's story spoke of a man from Lydia. That was an actual place in Greece. The story says that this man, this Gyges, was a shepherd who came upon a cave. Inside that cave was a tomb of a bronze horse who wore a golden ring. Gyges pocketed the ring and later discovered it made him invisible."

"This sounds like Lord of the Rings," said Percy. "You know when Frodo gets the One Ring."

"That wasn't Frodo," said Tristan. "It was the uncle, Bilbo."

"But Bilbo stole the ring from Golem," said Geraint.

"Oh, right," said Tristan.

"Hey," I said. "How come they get to talk out of turn?"

"As I was saying," said Geraint, cutting me off again. "Once this Gyges learned what the ring could do, he snuck into the palace, killed the king, and married the queen. Or he seduced the queen, and then killed the king, and took the throne. Whichever the order, all are equally bad."

"What happened to the ring?" asked Tristan.

"No one knows," said Geraint. "It doesn't come up again in any of Plato's stories. But it also doesn't look like Gyges used it again. Now there are rumors of the ring resurfacing in some competition. It's tied to Baros's name as he was asking about it."

"But your informant has no idea where Baros is now?" said Arthur.

Geraint shook his head.

"Nor do we know who this Gyges, if it's the same man, is?"

Geraint turned his palms up showing he had nothing else. All the knights looked around, but no one offered any more commentary. Finally, I raised my hand.

"Loren," sighed Arthur, "I've already said you don't have to raise your hand."

"I just wanted to make sure it was my turn to speak if no one else has anything else to add." I looked around the room at the mute men.

"You've already said you don't know where your lover is," said Geraint.

"Ex," I corrected. "And no, I don't know where Baros is. But I do know someone else in connection with this Gyges story, and I know where he is."

"You know Gyges?" asked Lance.

"No," I said. "I know Plato. Well, I don't know him like that. Nia was good friends with Socrates, and Socrates and Plato were like brothers, and I'm Nia's bestie, so I'm sure that makes us related in some kind of way."

The men all looked confused.

"Anyway, I know where Plato is. If I ask him, I'm sure he'd shed more light on his story. Maybe give us some clues as to who Gyges is and where the ring came from or ended up."

"Plato's dead," said Tristan.

"Nope," I said. "He's very much alive. He's a Chosen of the Greek Gods."

"You think the Olympians will grant you an audience with one of their Chosen?" asked Arthur.

"Of course," I said. "I helped to send their psycho dad back to the underworld. We're all, like, super tight now."

Arthur twirled the edge of his beard around his index finger. He pursed his lips as he considered me. It was his thinking face. His decision could go either way. I decided to give a little push in my favor.

"So, should I get Gwin to hook me up with a ley line transport to Athens?"

Arthur continued to twirl, and then finally he gave a curt nod. You could've knocked me over with a feather. I would've sworn I'd have to argue for days. But nope. I got a nod.

"Go and talk to Plato," he said. "Gather intel and see where it leads."

"You got it, boss."

It was going to be my first quest. Well, the first sanctioned quest. I was going to do amazing.

"But you're not going alone," said Arthur.

My gaze immediately connected with Gawain's. He gave me a smile of assent. He might not get down with me horizontally, but I knew he wasn't averse to some vertical action in the field.

"You'll take Geraint with you," said Arthur.

And just like that, my elation deflated.

6

Though I didn't subscribe to romantic love for myself, I couldn't get enough of the familial love. This brand of love I understood and wrapped around me like a fur coat in a snowstorm. I loved my new family. Like for reals.

My heart would swell when the kids came up to me chanting *Lady Lo* and asking me to teach them something that would tick their parents off. When their parents inevitably witnessed their kids' new inappropriate habit and discovered whom the children got it from, they did, in fact, get ticked off at me. But it would only be fleeting. Then they'd laugh and hug me to them like I was one of their own.

Because I was.

Theirs.

And they were mine.

I waved to Lady and Sir Hawthorne as they strolled toward the castle. Little Nigel Crissman ran a few circles around me before hugging my legs and then taking off into the back door of the kitchen. A few other townsfolk stopped me as I headed away from the castle as they made their way toward it.

It was dinnertime. Meals were a community affair here in Camelot. I walked against the flow as what appeared to be the entire town made its way into the dining hall. After years of being lost in the crowd, I was surrounded. Every day I was never want for company.

Day in and day out there were tons of tea invitations. These were all residents of the United Kingdom inside our own little town. Therefore, British mannerisms reigned supreme and pinkie fingers rose like clockwork early each evening as the people sipped their hot beverages.

There were weekly, sometimes daily, shopping sprees galore. This was a town populated by more women and witches than men, wizards, and knights. If we women weren't shopping, we could often be found watching sappy shows and chick flicks, saturating the town with even more estrogen.

There was training throughout the day with the

squires who each had a special place in my heart. Well, aside from Baysle, who still just rubbed me the wrong way and vice versa.

When training was over, I tended to my knightly business at the Round Table. Which was a lot of talking and reporting and more talking and strategizing. Men liked their war strategies.

My evenings were often occupied by the other two Galahad girls. Gwin and Morgan and I became thick as thieves from day one. We'd gossip and cackle in one of our bedrooms like a real coven.

I loved every minute of it. But it was also suffocating at times. Solitude had once been a friend of mine, and I often missed it.

I, alone, was left outside the castle once the meal service began. Looking up at the darkening sky, I inhaled before heading toward my destination. When I needed a moment to breathe, I always headed down to the stables.

"Good evening, my lady."

"Hey, Achila."

My magical mare bowed her head in greeting. The other horses raised their heads from their bales of hay and did the same, but they remained mute. Talking to humans was a chore the dams and stallions performed only when necessary. Whenever I rode Achila, it was often quiet. We both preferred the sound of the wind, and the beating of her hooves, to conversation.

Achila trotted toward the rack of saddles. "Might I offer you the pleasure of a ride?"

"You know my heart."

I mounted Achila, and we took off into the evening. The skies were awash in shades of blue from light periwinkle where the clouds tucked in the sun, to cobalt where the trees touched the horizon. The moon lit the way as we raced past the ancient Roman fort towards the river. As the dark blue shadows moved across the earth and sky, my mind wandered.

I couldn't help but wonder what Baros might want with a ring that granted invisibility. For a man who prided himself on his appearance and physique and his martial prowess, I doubted he could keep himself from adoring eyes for too long. Maybe he wanted to hide from the Olympians after trying to raise their filicidal father?

But that couldn't work. Zeus held Baros's soul. The Greek god could call Baros back to him with a simple thought.

When Nia and I had left Athens, after the adventure of locating Demeter's fabled tablet, Zeus was preoccupied with making up with his sister-wife, Hera. From what I knew, they were still making up. But what would happen when Zuzu and Hera (she didn't have a nickname which I always assumed led to her ire with her siblings) patched up their incest? Would Zeus call Baros's soul to the carpet? Would the golden god unravel Baros's spirit and send him to the afterlife?

As we raced across the moors, a pain radiated from my chest. I signaled Achila to slow down as my heart began to pound. She slowed and the wind slapped me in the face. I turned my face to the side and felt the wind change course, as though it were trying to smack sense upside my head.

I pulled Achila's reins, bringing us to a stop, and dismounted. We'd been riding along the water's edge of the River Usk. I knelt down at the river and splashed cold water on my face.

It must've been the magic in the waters that cooled me off. It slowed my racing heart. It also brought me to my senses.

I had no business feeling sorry for that man. I was a hero now with heroine responsibilities. My duty and my vows were to protect the weak and defenseless, to live by honor and seek justice, and ... A whole bunch of other things.

The list of the chivalric code was really, really long. I couldn't be expected to remember it all. I still couldn't remember the entire Girl Scout code, which is probably why I'd never graduated past a Brownie.

The point was that Baros had made a choice. The wrong choice. I wasn't going to break my long list of vows for him—especially when he'd never made any promises to me.

Don't get me wrong, this wasn't revenge. It was my job. I'd catch him, then hand him over to the authorities to mete out any punishment, but not before I got my questions answered and got my closure with him.

My stomach grumbled, twisting itself into a knot. It had to be hunger. I'd missed dinner because I wanted some solitude. I called Achila, and we headed back to the castle. The mare left me to dismount at the kitchen doors and made her way back to the stables.

I entered the kitchen to the smell of good food. Well, it smelled good to my nose. I knew no one else would want the dish. Igraine was often cooking the old-time meals. But I was one of few who would actually eat them.

Tonight she'd made garum. It was a fermented sauce made of fish intestines, blood, salt, and herbs.

She'd let the dish sit out at the window to get some sun. In the past, medieval folks would let it sit out for up to three months to get good and yummy. I hadn't had this since I was a kid. My mom would only ever make it when my dad wasn't at home. For some reason, it assaulted his nose. Not mine. I dug in.

"I hear you're going on your first quest in the morrow," Igraine said.

Her white hair framed her round face. Igraine was over a thousand years old but didn't look a day over seventy. I was pretty sure she was the oldest person in all of Camelot. And she showed no signs of slowing down.

I nodded in answer to her question instead of speaking around a mouthful of food.

"I would've thought you'd be happy," she said. "But I sense your heart is heavy."

Igraine was an empath. She could sense feelings, and also the path of a person' past, and the trajectory of their future. But her powers were often beyond her control. Sometimes, she saw things she'd rather not bear witness to. Personally, I wasn't particularly interested in having this conversation.

"The man we're tracking, he and I used to..."

"You loved him."

I held up my hands to ward off that word which people kept throwing at me. "I wouldn't go that far."

Igraine only offered me a knowing smile.

"We were fond of each other," I conceded. "But he never loved me."

"Love is never equal. There's always a trade. But if the tide is constantly low, you should lift the anchor. Your parents crashed into each other. I've never seen a love like that. Well, other than Arthur, the first, and Mara. Come to think of it, I remember Nia had a paramour. He looked at her like she'd pulled down the moon. What was his name?"

I knew instantly who she was talking about. "Zane."

"Yes, that's him. It was clear he loved her more than she did him, but not by much. I sense they will come to an equilibrium sometime in the future."

Sucked for Tres Mohandis, the guy who was currently trying to pull Nia into an even current of affection.

"First loves are hard," said Igraine. "They are the ones you expect to last. If the love fades, then the doubt takes root. The next attempt at love isn't often as strong with the tendrils of doubts now present in the heart. But even with the doubt that first love never dies. Just look at Gwin and Lancelot."

It was obvious that Gwin and Lance held a torch for each other, even though they tried to hide it. Zane didn't hide the way he felt about Nia. It was written all over his face when he looked at her. It was in his art as he painted each stroke of her form. He'd shout out his feelings to anyone who'd listen.

No one had ever done that for me. And, hey, it was cool. I wasn't that type of girl anyway.

"It wasn't love," I insisted. "Between me and Lenny."

Igraine looked at me knowingly, but she didn't argue. "It's very unsatisfying when you want to take a dip in the waters, but the tide is low. It's equally irksome to be drowned by a crushing wave of surf."

Both instances sounded pathetic to me. I didn't want to be shallow or drowned. I just like immersing my body in water from time to time. And I wasn't talking about the ocean, if you know what I mean.

"Call the water whatever you like," said Igraine. "But just like water changes states, that feeling of new love never truly fades, especially the first time you experience it."

I wasn't sure if that comforted me or not. Did I want Baros to return to me? Did I think he could turn good? I know there was good in him. Hell, look at me. I'd played the villain for a good portion of my life. Now I was reformed ... where it counted. Maybe when I found him, I could turn him to the light side of the force.

Hell, I probably could. I just needed to be sure and stay away from his lightsaber. That always screwed me up.

"Loren, dear, just remember the path we travel doesn't matter. It's the decisions you make along the way."

Igraine's words felt prophetic. Likely because she was a seer. I knew that her words would come back around. Hopefully, they came back to give me a helping leg up and not bite me in the ass.

7

———

"You got everything you need?" asked Morgan.

"I think so." I placed my father's satchel inside the hard shell of a suitcase. I usually traveled with only the soft pack, but ley line travel could sometimes end with a person waist deep in waters, and I didn't want my things to take an unnecessary bath.

"Wish I were going with you," said Morgan.

I shook my head. "That did not go so well the last time we went off on an adventure together."

She scowled, but I noted it wasn't at me. Arthur had made his way into the Throne Room accompanied by Geraint and Lance. The tension in the air thickened as Morgan stepped behind me, and Arthur stepped in front of me. I expected a war, but neither drew up arms. It was a rare calm day between those two.

"Where's Gwin?" Arthur asked.

"She was in the infirmary," I said.

A low growl came. I didn't look over to see from whom. I knew it came from Lance. Gwin was tending to Merlin, who was doing a remarkably slow job of dying.

"I'm here." Gwin came into the Throne Room. There were bags under her eyes, and she moved sluggishly.

"She can't make this trip," said Lance.

"Of course I can," she insisted.

Lance's features gentled along with his voice as he stepped closer to her. "You're tired."

Gwin's lips parted as she looked up at him. It was as though time stopped, and the violins played as the two regarded each other with care and attentiveness. But it was over just as soon as it began.

"I'm needed," Gwin said. "It's my duty."

Lance grit his teeth as she stepped around him. But he said nothing more. Just took up sentry behind her.

Gwin raised her hands. She began a chant, her

voice quiet and hoarse. I felt a tiny buzz of magic build, but as she flicked her finger, the magic only fizzled. Gwin sighed.

Her gaze caught Lance. He didn't wear an I told you so smirk. Instead, he looked at her with that same gentle care. His eyes seemed to implore her to take it easy.

Gwin turned to me and Geraint, resignation on her face. "Do you think you can delay your trip for a few hours? I just need a nap."

"She needs more than a nap," said Lance. "She needs some time off to rest."

I expected Gwin to argue. In fact, she opened her mouth. But no words of contradiction escaped her lips. No one was more shocked than Lance when she gave a slight nod of her head.

"Why don't I try to open a ley portal?" I asked.

The room had been quiet a second ago at Gwin's pronouncement, but you could hear a pin drop when I offered up my magic.

"I have enough magic," I said. "I just need some guidance on wielding it."

Gwin came to stand beside me. She directed me to lift my hands and focus my mind until I could feel the energy behind the door. I could feel it, rushing at me like a huge wave. It built and built. It was too late when I realized that wasn't a good thing.

"Pull back, Loren."

But I didn't know how. I felt the magic in my fingertips. I figured I could shake some off, like excess salt spilled on the table. I was wrong.

The magic left my body through my hands and crashed into the wall. But the crash happened from behind the door. The hinges flew off, and the door flew into the Throne room. All that was left was a hole where there had been a doorway.

"Why don't we just book a flight?" I said. "We'll be there by the evening."

The sun was low in the sky as our plane took off. I pushed the button to recline my seat the whopping two inches granted. Beside me, Geraint gripped the seat rest. He'd chosen the aisle seat, which didn't bother me. I loved looking out the window during takeoff and watching the world recede away.

I turned to Geraint. "I take it you don't like air travel?"

His brown skin looked green. The arches in his

eyebrows had flattened. "Magic, I trust. Machinery, not so much."

I released my seatbelt and turned to him. "You know Ger—"

"Buckle yourself back in." His voice was loud and reverberated off the cabin walls.

I turned with a smile and did as he said. "I didn't know you cared."

"I'm responsible for you now. It would reflect badly on me if you were thrown about during turbulence." His voice sounded more annoyed than cautionary.

"I think we got started off on the wrong foot," I said. "Why don't we try again."

"Try what again?"

"Getting to know each other," I said. "Becoming friends."

He didn't respond immediately. He took a moment to roll his eyes before he opened his mouth. And then we hit a pocket of air. Geraint gripped the seat again, his brown knuckles losing their color with the strength of his hold.

"Okay," I said. "I'll go first. Tell me about your parents?"

"They're both dead," he said through gritted teeth.

"What a coincidence. So are mine."

I waited for him to respond. He didn't. He didn't appear to get how this getting to know you thing worked.

"So, I gathered that your father was the last Sir Geraint?"

When I looked to him, he was taking a deep breath. Slowly, his fingers unfolded from the armrest now that the turbulence had stopped.

"What's your real name?" I asked.

He raised an eyebrow at me. I learned that knights were pretty possessive of their knighted names and all but eschewed their birth names when they claimed the seat. So far, I'd only gotten Arthur's real name and that was only under the duress of Banduri encroaching upon Camelot.

"Was your mother a witch?" I asked.

He sighed in answer.

"Mine too. Another coincidence."

Geraint turned and glared at me, but I was undaunted. We would be spending the next few days together. I would break him down.

"I'm an only child," I said. "What about you?"

"Two brothers."

I was surprised he offered. "Wow, two younger brothers."

"I'm the youngest," he corrected.

Another surprise. I would have assumed that the title went to the oldest son. But then again, Arthur was the younger brother of Merlin. The sword had passed over Merlin and chose Arthur to wield it.

I assumed it might be a sore point with Geraint's brothers that their youngest brother had been chosen. Couldn't hurt to ask. I wasn't doing well penetrating his armor so far anyway.

"How do your brothers feel about their baby brother taking the title?"

"One's dead. The other is ..."

He didn't finish the sentence. Which of course made me all the more curious. But I decided to table that until we were bosom buddies, which, given my calculations, would happen in about seventy-five years or so at this rate.

"Do you believe men and women can be platonic friends? I'm only asking because I have to assume that's the reason you're not opening up to me. Maybe you have a thing for me?"

"Maybe I just don't like you," he said.

I let out a trill of laughter. "Nonsense. Everybody likes me. And that includes you. If you didn't, you wouldn't have saved me back during the Battle of the Banduri."

"You mean the battle between your old school friends?"

Ouch. He had me there. "Let the record show that I extended friendship to them. They threw the first punch."

"Didn't they slap your offer of friendship down with a toxic bluestone? That's informative."

I glared at him.

"Did you ever consider that maybe I just want to sit here quietly?"

I shook my head. "When you sat quietly, you were tense. You're completely relaxed now."

Geraint blinked. Then he frowned. He looked down at his hands. They were no longer gripping the armrest.

"Admit it," I said. "My pestering you is relaxing."

He scrunched up his face and pursed his lips as though he were unwilling to let any admission pass through.

"Next topic on Loren and Geraint's epic journey into bromance; music. Who's your favorite band?"

His jaw tensed. I thought he wasn't going to answer. But then he did. "I like masinko music."

"I've never heard of that band."

"It's not a band. It's a musical instrument. Much

like a guitar. Here," he pulled out a handheld device, "why don't you have a listen?"

He shoved the headphones over my ears. I think he may have thought that would shut me up. Boy, was he in for a surprise.

8

I know Geraint's intentions were to shut me up. Or at least turn me off with the masinko music. But instead, I was enchanted. We shared his earbuds and listened to four whole albums by the time we touched down in Greece.

I wasn't fooled into thinking we were now best friends. But at least he wasn't sneering at me. Well, not any more than normal. And I had managed to get his Twitter handle and Facebook profile name while glancing at his phone. But he had yet to follow me or approve my friend request.

Once we'd claimed our bags and stepped outside the airport, Geraint hailed a taxi. He opened the door and handed me inside while the driver put our luggage in the belly of the trunk. I watched the dark knight fold his form into the backseat of the car and a crinkle creased my brow.

The first time I saw this man was atop a horse when I'd first come into the town of Camelot. He'd been an imposing figure with this chin high and his nose angled down. He'd glanced at me the same way the airport security guards had when we'd boarded. When Geraint's gaze landed on my breasts, it wasn't to ogle. He'd scanned for possible concealed weapons, looking for anything that might pose a threat to the people under his charge. Once I'd passed his scan, he'd ignored me and leaned back in his saddle, ever watchful for the next possible threat.

He sat next to me now, at eye level. Even though there was a cushion at his back, he sat up straight as though he were in a saddle. His eyes scanned the interior of the car as well as its driver. This knight's guard was never down.

I looked out the window, watching as the city of Athens came into clear view. Like Camelot, the city was a harmonious blend of classical and contemporary. The glistening rocks of the temples of the gods dominated the cold steel of the tall towers of modern man.

As a kid, I remembered running through the ruins, which were a maze of rocks and steel as efforts were underway to save them. Most of my days were spent at the Parthenon as my father consulted the reconstruction efforts. It was late afternoon now and the sun lit the aged temple. The Parthenon looked like a bionic shrine with metallic reinforcements holding together its crumbling, marble flesh.

That building had survived wars, explosive blasts, and botched restoration attempts. I understood what it was like being on the wrong side of an invading force. I knew what it felt like to be a waylay station and to be used as a shelter, as well as a shield. I knew all too well how the earth could shake when relationships went south. But the current restorers looked as though they knew what they were doing. I had a feeling their reinforcements would hold 'til the end of time.

"Are you ready, my lady?"

I looked to Geraint. He held his hand out to me. The taxi had stopped, and we were at our destination. I took his hand and climbed out of the car. Even though trust was a thin layer between Geraint and I, he was everything that was chivalrous and gentlemanly. He opened the door for me. He carried my satchel. I'd forgone the hard suitcase since we traveled by air, and it was unlikely we'd end up in a lake.

As I slung my bag over my shoulder, I remembered the last time I was here with my real bestie, Nia. We'd arrived by private yacht that time, the yacht of billionaire Tresor Mohandis. Which reminded me, I needed to call her and see what was up between the two of them. The last time we spoke, she was being tugged between Tres and Zane. Whichever direction she picked, she couldn't go wrong. Both men would lay down their life for her.

I had that now. The knights were six musketeers. Meaning they were one for all and all for one; now all for seven. But none of them looked at me the way Tres and Zane both looked at Nia. Baros had never looked at me like that either.

Oh sure, he'd looked at me with lust, and there was pride mixed in there at my abilities. And yeah, he was often amused by me, I was an amusing girl. But devotion? I'd only ever seen that reflected in his opaque eyes when I'd looked at him.

"Are we expected?" asked Geraint as we headed towards the elevator.

"I'm an old friend," I said as I punched in the code I remembered seeing Lenny punch in when he took me up to the Olympians' penthouse. "It's all good."

Before the doors to the elevator closed, I gave a

finger waggle to a sheet of hotel stationery. It glided its way on the floor, barely missing a few stilettos and boots before sliding into the closing elevator doors, and slipping past Geraint's notice. Barely.

I saw his brow quirk. His gaze flitted left and then right and then at me. I offered him a smile, which made him all the more suspicious. But he couldn't pinpoint the root of his suspicions, and he let it go.

With the piece of stationery in my left hand, I slipped a pen out of my pocket and scrawled a note behind my back. When the doors opened to the penthouse, the way was blocked by big, burly men with opaque eyes.

Chosen guards. Likely real live gladiators from the time of the Coliseum. The Olympians liked to keep it old school.

"Hi," I said to the Chosen gathered outside the Olympians' private apartments. "I'm Loren, remember me? I kinda saved the world a couple of months ago. You know, from when Hera tried to raise the Titans?"

They stared blankly at me, which was easy since they didn't have pupils. I couldn't tell if I'd met any of them before. They honestly all looked alike to me.

"Here," I said, producing the note from behind my back. "I'm expected."

One man took the note. I knew he was reading it though I couldn't see his eyes scanning left to right. Once he was done, he looked over his shoulder and gave a head nod, indicating that the other man should read the note.

"Old friend, huh?" asked Geraint.

I saw his hand itch for his sword. Our swords were magical and easily evaded airport detection as they could take on another shape. I laid a hand on his sword arm to ease his trigger finger.

"The goddess didn't say she was expecting anyone," said one Chosen.

"But this is her handwriting," said another Chosen.

Of course it was, I wanted to huff. I was an excellent forger. In my youth, I'd copied some of the greatest paintings around. Mimicking someone's chicken scratch was a poor use of my talents.

It was a talent I'd likely inherited from my mother, along with my witch's blood. My mother never forged anything, but her paintings were incredibly lifelike. Probably because of the magic pooling at her fingertips.

The Chosen warriors shrugged and began

toward a door. I smiled congenially at Geraint. His brow told me that he knew something was up. We were almost home free when I heard a door open.

"Guards, I need one of you to take out the trash."

I knew that voice. A rack of new clothing was shoved out of her door. I could still see some price tags dangling from the unworn clothes. My mouth salivated over what she considered trash, and my palms itched to grab.

"Yes, my goddess," said one of the Chosen. "And your visitor is here."

"Visitor?" Demeter poked her dark head out of the door.

"A Ms. Van Alst," said the Chosen.

Shrewd, light eyes that filled with ire looked me up and down. Demeter cocked her head to the side. Then she ran a pink claw down the side of her face. "Who?"

It was the ultimate diss. I clamped down on my tongue and inhaled a lungful of patience. Yeah. It didn't work.

"Poor thing must be going senile," I said. "She's like five thousand years old."

Demeter's eyes glistened hot fire. So, of course, I went in for the kill.

"You remember me, Demi. I'm Loren Van Alst, Nia's best friend."

Her eyes narrowed. "Everyone knows I'm Nia's best friend. Like I said, take out the trash."

The men turned back to me and produced an array of weapons. The first brought forth a thick, iron blade. Another, a javelin. And the third began swinging a spiked flail.

I sighed. "You know Nia will get pissed if you harm a hair on my pretty, blonde head."

"You're a temporary pet. She'll have forgotten you by the next century. She always does with her human pets."

"Jealousy looks good on you, Demi. Green is so your color."

Demeter rolled her eyes and snapped her fingers. The men advanced. Geraint stepped up side by side with me. In this, at least, I was his equal.

"Stop."

The men halted at Demeter's command.

Ha? Had she seen reason? Wait, no. That wasn't likely.

A salacious smile crossed Demeter's lips. She sashayed through the Chosen who parted for her. Running one of her painted claws over her lip, she darted out her tongue as though she were going to take a taste.

I didn't swing that way, but it sure did boost a girl's confidence. My mind was spinning on how to let her down gently when she walked past me and turned her back on me. She came face to face with Geraint.

"What do we have here?" she said. "What is that I smell? It's an ancient spice I haven't come across in centuries. Is that …? Could it be …? Chivalry?"

Geraint lowered his sword, mesmerized by the goddess. I watched his fingers twitch around the hilt of his sword. His throat muscles worked.

"Sir Geraint, at your service," he said.

"A knight?" Demeter twittered.

Geraint's grin spread even wider.

I cleared my throat. "That's my brother."

"She's not my sister," he said.

"Am so. 'Cause I'm a knight, too," I said.

"A complete fluke in the system," said Geraint.

"Dude!"

"I don't know why Nia put up with her," said Demeter. "She seems as annoying as a stray; tagging along behind you, begging for scraps off your table, pawing all over your things."

"Exactly," said Geraint.

"I'll get rid of her," said Demeter. "Wanna come take your armor off and show me your sword?"

"I could've sworn we were on a mission or something?" I came behind Demeter, right in Geraint's line of sight. He squinted at me. I watched him struggle to come back to his senses under the onslaught of Demeter's powers.

"I'm responsible for Lady Loren." The words looked as though they pained Geraint to say. "Another time perhaps. Right now, we need your help"

"Fine," Demeter said. "What can I do for you and Laura?"

I let it slide. Being grown up was hard work. "We're looking for Baros."

"Aw." Demeter regarded me pitifully.

Let it slide, Laura. Let it slide. "I don't want him back or anything. I'm looking to get a ring."

Demeter's head cocked to the other side looking down on me as though I were pathetic.

"Bad choice of words." I held up my hands. "Let me start again—"

"We believe Baros is after a magical object called the Ring of Gyges," said Geraint. "The object, if in the wrong hands like Baros's, could pose a great threat to the world. We're on a mission to retrieve it."

"Baros isn't here," said Demeter. "We haven't heard hide nor hair of him since Eleusis."

"Is Zeus here?" I asked. "Surely he can pinpoint him as Baros is his chosen."

"Zuzu is off being, well, Zuzu."

"We understand that one of your devoted, Plato, wrote about the ring," said Geraint. "Perhaps we can speak with him instead, ask him some questions?"

"Of course," said Demeter. "I'll take you to my sister, Tia's offices."

She looped her arm through Geraint's and headed to the elevator leaving me tagging along in their wake.

9
____

The sun was sinking down into the horizon as we climbed into Demeter's town car. The scattering molecules in the atmosphere bruised the canvas of the sky. The clouds swelled in violent purples and pinks.

The temples lit up the night in all their aged glory. The fluorescent lights took on a golden gleam making it appear as though the gods had returned to their dwellings for the night. But the gods were not asleep in their tombs. They were wide awake and getting on my last nerve.

"Oh, I suppose you can sit back here with us," Demeter said as I slid into the seat across from her in the rear of the luxury.

The last time I'd been in a car with her, it was as

we raced across town to stop an acropolytic apocalypse. I'd sat up front with Baros. It hadn't occurred to me that I might be looked down upon as the help. I'd just wanted to be with my lover. Tres and Nia had sat together in the back. Demeter and Bet, another Immortal like Nia, had sat in a huddle too. The two had a torrid history.

"Where's your boyfriend?" I said to Demeter.

A barely noticeable tick quivered at the corner of her right eye. On the other side of her face, her left jaw tensed. Demeter sniffed as she crossed her arms beneath her boobs. "Boyfriend? Such a childish term."

I tried to hold my features expressionless. I knew the term was childish. Had I not said that just the other day?

"I don't have those," said Demeter. "I have men who are devoted to me. Women, too."

"Oh," I said. "So, there is nothing going on between you and Bet? Good to know. He's a looker."

Demeter's eyes sparkled with the fire of thousands of souls. I sat bolt straight. My body angled toward her of its own accord, almost like I was bowing. To her.

The Olympian gods lived off the souls of willing humans. But it hadn't always been like that. The

Titans, their parents, had eaten humans whole, taking their souls forcibly and making the surviving humans their slaves. Demons, these soul-slaves were called. Instead of the opaque eyes of the willing and devoted Chosen, demons' eyes were black and hollow because their souls had been ripped from them against their will.

The Olympians had outlawed the practice, but they still had the power to do it. I suspected Demeter had put a little demonic spice on Geraint earlier in the hall when she'd gazed at him. Though looking at him now, I would have to admit that she wouldn't have needed to add much. Geraint was reserved but willing.

But me? I'd given this goddess my soul willingly before. I didn't have a choice. It had been a better-the-devil-you-know situation. Either I let Demeter hold my soul willingly or have it taken by her demented sister, Hera, as she'd tried to raise her homicidal father.

Demeter had given me my soul back after the battle in Eleusis. But I always suspected she'd shifted things around in there. And now I saw that she still had a pinkie-finger hold on me as my body tried to bend to her will, literally.

I gave myself an internal shake and felt her hold

break. I narrowed my eyes at her. She grinned wickedly. Then she blinked in surprise.

"So, you're a witch now? I didn't know they gave out magic to just anyone these days."

"I was always a witch," I said. "I just didn't know it. Now, I do. So keep your eyes to yourself."

Geraint leaned into me, looking between me and Demeter. "You two are friends, you said?"

"Oh, my dear sir, I don't friend the help," said Demeter. "She's Nia's ... associate. I thought Nia was in England with you lot."

"Nia is in the States," I said. "You would know that if you were best friends."

Before Demeter and I could start another catfight, the car came to a stop. Geraint stepped out when the driver opened the door. The knight handed out Demeter and then me. I tried not to let the order that we departed the car rankle but, if I was honest, I'd started keeping score. And she was now ahead. I glared at Geraint as he handed me out of the car. His brows drew together in the universal man language of 'What did I do?'

We entered a building that could have been an ancient temple with its columns and porticos. Except they were all made of steel and glass. The doors opened automatically. Once inside, it was impossible not to feel the hum of electricity running along the wires.

The people on the floor moved as fast as the World Wide Web. They all were plugged in with headsets and handhelds. There was a mashup of fashion from men in draped togas and tailored suits to women in flowing peplos and designer skirts. What all of them had in common were their opaque eyes.

I saw a statue of Atlas holding the world on his shoulders. There was priceless artwork and paintings all over the walls. But more prominently featured were whiteboards with complex mathematical problems.

I'd heard about this place. It was the world's most exclusive, most sought after collection of think tanks. These were all the chosen of the goddess, Hestia. She loaned out humanity's greatest minds to solve problems as mundane as farming and ending world hunger to curing cancer and finding dark matter.

The workers on the floor noticeably went into a faster-paced tizzy as a brown-skinned woman with cropped hair marched down the hall. She held two tablets in one hand with a phone pressed to her ear with the other hand. She spoke into the phone as she tapped her thumb on the top handheld. She never once looked up. Neither did she bump into anyone or anything as she came closer to us. That wasn't so surprising. She was a goddess, after all.

Hestia came to a halt before her sister. "What are you doing here, Demi? Is it another sister bonding day?" Her face crumpled as she looked at her varied devices.

"No, Tia. It's—"

"Good," Hestia sighed. "Because I felt like we just had one. Really you're taking Hera's mishap too far. I don't see why I have to suffer."

"Tia, I'm here because—"

But Hestia held up her hand, actually it was just her index finger. The other four were still wrapped around her tablets. Hestia hadn't once looked up at her sister during their little heart-to-heart.

"Ari, Thag?" said Hestia.

"Yes, my goddess?" Two older men stepped forward. I'd seen them the first time I was here in Athens with Nia. I knew they were Aristotle and Pythagoras. "I need one of you to answer this correspondence from the World Bank. It seems the Euro is slipping again."

"We're on it, my goddess," said the white-haired Ari.

Hestia made to move around her sister, but Demeter grabbed her arm. "Tia."

Finally, Hestia looked up and directly at her sister. "You don't have to yell, Demi. Just say you want my attention. What is it?"

Demeter let out a huff of air. "We're looking for Plato."

"Whatever for? Are you and Bet on the outs again? You haven't had a thing for philosophers for centuries."

"Not for me. For them." Demeter jerked her thumb over her shoulder at me and Geraint.

I waved my fingers in greeting to Hestia. Geraint gave a courtly bow of his head.

"I've hired Plato out as a jury consultant," said Hestia. "He's on the helipad about to take off."

Geraint and I looked at each other, then we looked up to the ceiling.

"Is there an elevator?" Geraint asked.

Hestia pointed. Geraint and I shoved ourselves into the metal box. It ticked away slowly up four flights until it reached the roof. We sprang forth once the doors released us.

The chopper's wings had just begun to spin as we came upon the helipad. We waved down the pilot. When he paid us no heed, I summoned a magical fireball with my hands and tossed it into the air.

I'd meant to toss it in front of the copter. Unfortunately, my aim wasn't so good, and it hit the nose of the conveyance. Beside me, Geraint sighed. I could only shrug my shoulders. Technically, I'd accomplished what we raced up here to do. The engine of the plane cut, and the blades came to a halt. The doors to the chopper opened, and a pale-haired, wiry thin man peered out.

"Plato?" I asked.

He nodded.

"We need your help. We're looking for Baros."

Plato's pale eyes darkened ever so slightly. There were externally visible signs of an inner war as the philosopher of morality struggled with his blood-lust. Baros had participated in the stolen death of his honored friend earlier this year. With Baros's help, Hera had stolen Socrates's soul and made him a demon.

Plato climbed out of the helicopter and walked to the side of the roof with us. He looked over his shoulder before he spoke. "He's likely gone to ground. If Zeus were here, he could tell you, if it was his prerogative."

Now, I saw why he looked around. It was to make

sure he wasn't heard. It wouldn't do to disparage the brother of the goddess who held your soul in the cornea of her eyes.

"I know what Baros is after," I said. "If I can find the object, I can find him."

"I'll help in any way I can."

"What more can you tell me about the Ring of Gyges?"

10

"Socrates loved to hear himself talk. Imagine how thrilled he was when I wrote a book that was about his discussions." Plato laughed as he spoke. His pale eyes shone bright in the dawning moonlight as we stood atop the roof.

When Nia and I came here months back, it was during Socrates's wake. He was likely the only man in the history of the world to attend his own going home celebration. It had come as no great shock to his many friends. Socrates had been ready to pass on for some time. It had been his choice to move on from this world as he grew wary and weary of the new generation. In a time where information was so readily at hand and opinions were so wide and available at such a speed, he'd felt like the modern society was less and less like a democracy and more like a hive mind. He'd insisted that his usefulness was up, and so he decided to leave this world.

I'd attended his actual funeral, as had he. I'd watched as Hestia, with a glisten in her bright eyes, had returned the essence she'd imbibed back into Socrates's body. When his soul was returned, his pale eyes closed, and he fell down dead as hundreds of years caught up with him. But only an hour later, his eyes reopened, black as night, as a demon. Baros had helped to do that to him.

"Socrates's favorite topic was the meaning of justice; specifically, whether a just man is happier than an unjust man," Plato continued. "We were discussing this when it caught the ear of the one called Gyges."

"The shepherd?" I asked.

Plato shook his head. "He was no shepherd. He's not even a man. He's fae."

"Fae? As in fairies?" I turned to Geraint. "You didn't tell me they were real."

"They're from another realm," said Geraint. "They don't come to earth often. Mainly because they look down on humanity, but also because the doors aren't easy to pass through."

"There are cracks," said Plato. "Every once in a while, the fae come here for mischief."

"You mean like a Spring Break?" I asked.

"Gyges decided to test Socrates's theory of justice," said Plato. "People have long believed that *The Republic* was based on hypotheticals. The truth is, all the stories happened. Gyges put each of the debates to the test. He pitted friend against friend, sibling against sibling, even husband against wife. All for his cruel enjoyment."

Plato's pale gaze was haunted. But he shook himself.

"Why didn't you write that?" I asked.

"Fae are powerful creatures. They scrub all truth of their existence from human record. Most supernatural creatures and deities who don't care to be bothered by mankind do so. Gyges is a being you're better off not knowing."

"Can you tell us about the Ring of Invisibility?" I asked.

"Invincibility," corrected Plato. "It's the true story of how Polemarchus obtained his wealth. Gyges sent him into a cave. Inside the cave was a tomb with a bronze horse that contained a dead man. On the finger of the dead man was a golden ring—the Ring of Invincibility. The question posed was if no one could find out, and if you would not get punished, would you do an injustice? Polemarchus took the ring and asked it to grant him invisibility. Once he was no longer seen, he killed the richest man in Lydia whose wife he'd once loved. Polemarchus stole the man's fortune and no one was the wiser. Proving even a virtuous man had his vices."

"The moral being that crime pays?" I asked.

"For a time," said Plato. "Polemarchus was later executed during the political upheaval of the Thirty Tyrants after they stole the ring from him."

"So, the Tyrants have the ring?" asked Geraint.

"No," said Plato. "Gyges has it. The ring won't work unless you earn it in one of Gyges's tournaments. Baros has entered before and lost. He nearly lost his life trying to attain it."

"But why would Lenny want to become invisible?" I asked.

"Not just invisible," said Plato. "Invincible. With the ring, he could break the hold the gods have on him and never be brought to justice. Then I'm sure he'd turn his sights to Persia. As a Spartan, he's never gotten over that defeat."

Plato waved us back into the building. "It won't be too hard to find where he's holding the tournament. Magical beings like technology because they don't have to do any of the work."

We walked into a room that was decked out with high tech computers. The smell of coffee, sugar, and caffeine clung to my nose hairs making it hard to inhale. When the air finally got through my nasal passageways, I felt my brain light up like it had been hit by a ping pong ball.

Plato made his way over to a woman with skin the color of sand and the high cheekbones I'd only seen in Egyptian pyramids. All she needed was a tall crown, and she could've been Pharaoh Nefertiti.

"Hypatia," said Plato. "I need a favor."

The Hypatia? No way. I'd done a paper on her during my short stint in private school. She was from Alexandria, Egypt. She was believed to be the first female mathematician, but all her works were lost.

Luckily, she wasn't. Hypatia sat at a computer terminal that had funny symbols instead of letters and numbers on the keyboards. On the multiple screens were lines of code, which reflected in her translucent eyes.

"I'm busy hacking into North Korea's mainframe," she said. "They've made a bit of progress in their nuclear endeavors. I'm introducing a few kinks to set them back a couple of years."

"I just need a second of your time," said Plato.

"I'm kinda saving the world here," she said.

"It's to do with catching Baros."

Hypatia's fingers paused. She must've been close with Socrates, too. With a single press of a button, the screen blanked. "What do you need?"

"We're trying to determine where an underground, magical tournament might be being held. Likely in a remote area or on an ancient site."

Before Plato had finished talking, Hypatia's fingers were flying across the keyboard. Images and code flashed faster than my mind could comprehend.

"Aha," said Hypatia. "A lot of electricity is being used beneath the Roman Colosseum. Deliveries from Apple have been noted in the vicinity as well. It has to be there."

Which meant that Baros would be there. If Baros got the ring, he would be free of Zeus's control and wouldn't be dealt his hand of justice. Which would be bad because I was on the side of justice, not on the side of seeing my ex go free so that he could come groveling to me. I had my priorities totally straight.

"Loren!"

I turned my head to Geraint. It sounded like he'd been calling my name for a moment. "What?"

"Are you paying attention?" he asked.

"Of course," I said having not a clue as to what he'd said. "We're totes on the same page."

11

"You don't like flying. You don't trust my magic. This is the next best way."

I crossed my arms as I stared at Geraint. A fire blazed before us. Geraint stared at the flames, grimacing as they licked up the sides of the brick hearth. He planted his feet wide on the hard-wood floor and crossed his arms over his chest like a petulant child.

"I'm not getting into a fire," he said.

"It's perfectly safe," said Desi. "As long as you hold onto me."

The Greek god of the underworld leaned against the far wall. The orange flames shimmied in the palm of one of his tanned hands. The fingers of his other hand toyed with the ginger beard at his chin.

We'd left the think tank twenty minutes ago on our own. Demi had forced Tia into sister bonding time, dragging Hestia out to dinner for some quality time. Hestia had gone, kicking and screaming and clinging to all of her devices. As that drama played out, the Chosen had put us in touch with Desi to get us on our way to Rome sooner.

The middle son of the Titans was a noted Hollywood film producer. But you wouldn't know him if you saw him. He did his magic behind the scenes, mostly producing his brother, Poseidon's, children's books. Their most famous one was about a group of orphans who were the children of the gods and the hijinks they got into trying to save the world from mythical creatures. It was complete fiction as the Greek gods couldn't have children of their own, being that they weren't exactly human.

Anyway, though Desi worked in Cali, he lived in Athens. The flights back and forth would've been murder on his wallet, but he had an entirely different way of traveling. That was through fire. And where did humans keep most of their fire? In fireplaces, of course.

"I thought you said he was one of Arthur's knights," Desi said jabbing his thumb towards Geraint.

"He has trust issues," I said. "I'm working on them."

"I don't have trust issues," Geraint said. "I have intelligence. Walking through fire equals getting burned."

"It's like a ley line," Desi sighed. "You witches and knights go into a dark void with no problem. Walking through fire, works the same, just with less magic and more adrenaline."

"And a higher degree of temperature," mumbled Geraint.

Desi shrugged. "Gets me into far more places than a witch can travel. Fire is everywhere."

Geraint uncrossed his arms. He took a step forward. An ember escaped the fireplace and landed on a rug on the floor, burning a hole through the material. Geraint took two steps back.

"Listen," said Desi, "I'm all for helping you track Baros. Zeus may not give a damn, but I care about what happens to the people under my protection. I'm prepared to help get you closer to him...whenever you're ready."

I looked to Geraint, but his chin was still steely. I threw up my hands in exasperation. "I'm going to go through. You have to protect me as a witch. That means you have to follow me."

"I thought you were a knight," said Geraint.

"Witch? Knight? You label me conveniently depending on whether you want me to do something or not do something. Now, I'm doing the same."

I stepped up to the hearth and faced Desi. The god shrugged, kicking off the wall and coming to join me. We both turned and faced Geraint.

The knight balled his hands into fists. He scrunched his face up, making me certain this is what he'd look like as a young squire performing the undesirable duties he put the current batch of squires through. Finally, he shook out his hands, unscrunched his face, and joined me and Desi. Luckily, we hadn't needed to go back to the hotel since we each carried our luggage over our shoulders in satchels. Geraint adjusted his pack, holding the straps until the tension nearly snapped it in two.

I grinned up at him. "Look at it this way, if something goes wrong you get to blame it all on me and say I told you so."

"I'm more than certain that will happen before this is done," he said.

Before I could respond, the fire flared up. The flames lifted my hair and consumed us. Fire travel was nothing like ley travel. Ley travel was an energy exchange. Desi's fire took a bite out of me.

We stepped out on the other end. Geraint hopped out of the fireplace, patting his clothing and hopping around in his boots. I took note of his eyebrows and saw that they were singed. The fire had taken the edge off the points. It totally worked, and now I saw what the women of Camelot saw in him.

A feminine gasp broke my attention from the knight, and I focused on our surroundings. We'd turned up in a luxurious bedroom. A woman lounged on a four-poster, queen-sized bed. She lay naked, her pale skin drowning in deep, red sheets.

"Desi is that you?" She drawled in Italian. Her gaze fixed on me and then Geraint. "Naughty boy, you brought friends."

Desi turned to us and grimaced unapologetically. "Sorry. I was aiming for the formal living room's fireplace. But my mind was here in the bedroom. Just go down the stairs and out the door. I'm sure you'll find your way to the Colosseum."

Geraint and I turned to the door. The naked woman frowned as we headed toward the exit. Well, she frowned as Geraint headed toward the exit. She barely spared me a second glance. But her gaze quickly fell upon Desi, and the heat of desire between them burned brighter than the fire creeping up her chimney.

Geraint and I took the stairs to the first level, found the door, and spilled out onto the streets of Rome. Geraint shut the door behind us and then he turned to me. He glared for a full minute.

"I'm ready to say I told you so," he said.

"Nothing happened," I insisted.

He raised his brows, but the point was lost.

"In my opinion, that went really well. You came out the better for it." I reached for his brow, but he swatted my hand away. "Dude, now all the women will want you."

"I don't have any problems with women." Geraint shrugged past me and went into the street.

"Obviously." I fell in step with him. "I saw you and Percy with your little tag team game on knights' night out."

"Those women don't count. I'm not interested in something superficial and carnal. I'm looking for ..."

I waited with bated breath. "What?"

He clamped his mouth shut.

"Tell me. We're bonding here."

He sighed as we continued down the street. "You're not going to let this go, are you?"

"See, we *are* bonding. That's exactly what I'm not going to do."

Geraint sighed again. "My parents' marriage was arranged. But it worked. They made a commitment to each other, and they were happy."

"So, you want to be set up? Oh, let me do it!"

"That's not what I said." Geraint shook his head. "Besides, you don't know anything about me."

"Yes, I do," I said. "You're from Northern Africa originally, but you grew up in Victorian England where you've been in the cultural minority. Though no one in Camelot treated you differently, I'd be willing to bet whenever you stepped outside of the city grounds, people looked down their nose at you. I know you're special because a magical sword chose you above your two older siblings. But that also made you feel isolated in your family. You enjoy classical music, which tells me you're more of an introvert. That says to me that the girl for you will need a quiet strength and a strong sense of morality. She'll be someone who stands apart from the crowd but doesn't try to draw attention to herself. She'll be someone who understands your isolation in a crowd of people. How am I doing so far?"

I looked beside me and there was no one there. I turned around and Geraint was a few steps behind me staring at me. His eyes were wide with both disbelief and vulnerability.

"See." I grinned. "I listen. And I'm very intuitive. Do I get the job?"

He didn't answer. Instead, he picked up the pace. He didn't say another word until we were outside of the Colosseum. It was after hours, and the gates to the attraction were closed.

"Can your intuition tell us where the fight is and how to get in?" Geraint asked.

"As a matter fact, it can," I said. There was magic in the air, like a ley line but different. I couldn't quite put my finger on what I was feeling, but I knew it was supernatural. "I can feel magic underfoot."

My body felt like a homing fork. I began to walk around. Not using my sight, I was using that well inside me where my magic laid.

The magic down below called to me. It brought me to a stop at a grate in the street. I reached down to the circular piece of metal with my magic. My fingers spread, and a warmth spread through my palm.

I wasn't sure what I was doing, but my magic knew. The grate wiggled. Then it twisted. One more pull, and the circular disk flew up into the air, landing a few yards away.

Look at that. I'd opened a magical door. I did a little cheer and dance. I took a few steps toward the opening, and then I looked over my shoulder at Geraint.

He sighed, shrugged, and finally took a step forward. "*Carpe diem.*"

12

I've seen a lot of crazy things in my human life. I'd swam in the Devil's Pool in Zambia. Why was it called the Devil's Pool, you ask? Because it was the natural pool at the edge of Victoria Falls where the waters fell down a one hundred meter drop.

I'd walked on the same ice as an Arctic polar bear. I held my ground when the bear spotted me on the other side of the ice. I only took a step back when I heard the ice crack. I wasn't stupid.

And it wasn't like I'd never been to a boxing match or a martial arts bout. I'd been on the fencing circuit for all of my teen years. Hell, I'd even found my way into a couple of real-life fight clubs in New

York City. Though I can't talk about them because of the rules.

I'd seen crazier things during my adventures with Nia. There had been high-flying cannibal assassins of the Gongyi in China when we'd searched out dragon bones. Or that time we'd come to Greece not too long ago where we'd watched humans get their life essence sucked out through their eyeballs. Not to mention that I now lived in freaking Camelot with witches, knights, and talking horses.

All these wonders paled in comparison to what we walked into beneath the Colosseum.

"You told me dragons weren't real," I said.

"I never said that," said Geraint.

A dragon spread his wings and roared as a troll charged it. The dragon reared up on its hind legs, standing over ten feet tall. Its black wings spanned at least fifteen feet on either side. Its long, snake-like neck was the most beautiful emerald green I'd ever seen. I expected its head to be the pointy angles of a lizard or a snake, but it was shaped more like a hairless lion's with a proud jaw and a pug nose. The animal was simply beautiful.

It raised its sharp black talons and sliced downward. Red coated its nails as though it had just gotten a manicure. The bloody polish dripped onto the ground as though in need of an air dryer.

I admired the color of the glossy coat. I brought my own nails in front of my face as the dragon's opponent, the owner of that lush red liquid, roared in anger at the gashes on his chest.

The dragon faced off against what could only be described as a troll. It had three rows of teeth, two on the top and one on the bottom. There were a few jagged teeth missing here and there.

The troll was half the size of the dragon. Its fleshy body looked like it would make a tasty meal. Instead of cowering, the troll dug in its heels. Then it launched itself at the dragon. No one was more surprised than me when the troll piledrivered the dragon, upending the large beast and dropping it head first into the arena floor.

The crowd leapt up onto their feet and roared louder than the two beasts at center stage. We were beneath the Colosseum. I'm not sure how far down we'd traveled. One moment, we were on the streets and, the next moment, we were here in the underground space. I knew we were not exactly in Kansas, or maybe even Rome, anymore.

The amphitheater before Geraint and I was made of pristine marble that glistened under the bright lights. I didn't see a single light bulb or fluorescent tube. It was as though a sun lit the area to be a warm spring day.

Magic. It was all magic. But not like mine.

This was different. Older. Purer. Stronger. My fingers and toes were tingling, aching to reach out and touch it.

In the gathered crowd were beings of every color—and I don't mean human races. You know how people try to be inclusive and say they don't care if people are white, black, or purple. There were purple people here.

There were people with petals as wings. There were people with antennas reaching out of their heads. This one female, every time she moved, sparkles shook off her body like a cloud of baby powder.

"What are they?" I asked.

"Fae," said Geraint. "It's believed that they evolved from plants before humans evolved from primates."

The fae were all slender folks like wispy willows. They came in every shade of pastels like lavender, rose, and periwinkle. They looked like they were walking flowers and butterflies. But they cheered with the bloodlust of starved vampires.

On the arena floor, blood poured as the troll pummeled the dragon with its meaty fists. For a moment, the dragon just lay there and took the pounding. The troll began to tire as it tore at the rawhide. At the first lull in the troll's assault, the dragon blew a stream of fire that burned the troll to a crisp.

The crowd of dainty flower people went absolutely wild. The smell of burning flesh hit my nose from the nosebleed seats we'd walked into. Another plume of smoke rose from the far side of the arena as the troll's bones burned to a crisp and then sprinkled over the dragon's body.

The plume was not the dragon's. It was a rainbow of pastels. Sparks spread out of the clouds, twirling like dive-bombing sparkles. From the merry pyrotechnics emerged a male. I think?

His skin was pale purple—like lavender. His brows were the deep blue of Morning Glories. His lips were the pink blush of carnations. Gold sparkled at the edges of his eyes like magical mascara.

He was beautiful. But still masculine with a broad chest, strong thighs, and big hands. I couldn't help myself. I looked down.

Yup, big designer shoes. Complete with pinstripe

pants and a cream colored shirt with more ruffles and lace than should work. But it did.

The man spread his arms wide and tilted his head back to look up at the crowd. His stance, his outrageous clothing, and his colorful person reminded me of a circus ringleader.

"Thank you all for viewing our pre-show entertainment," he said.

That was the preshow?

The dragon limped off the arena stage. A chant rose up in the crowd. "Gyges! Gyges!" they shouted. It was him. The fabled Gyges. The fae king who liked to play games of morality and cunning.

"Do we have a show for you tonight," he said. "In this series of bouts for The Ring of Invincibility, you will witness battles of will, the unveiling of secret desires, the might of physical prowess, and the elasticity of mental fortitude, as we get to learn what lies in the hearts of men. So ..."

The crowd of fifty thousand was quiet, enough to hear a caterpillar fart. Gyges's grin widened as he held everyone at the edge of their seats. More pastel pyro exploded around the showman.

"Let's get ready to rumble," he shouted into the thin air without a microphone, but his voice boomed up into the corners of the highest crevices of the arena. "Up next, we have two contenders. The first has tumbled into debt. His house is on the line. If he doesn't win, his family will suffer."

A man walked into the ring. He looked fairly nondescript like he could've walked in from the streets. The man's eyes widened at the creatures assembled. It was clear he was human. He tripped as his feet brought him to his corner of the arena ring.

"And in this corner, our second contender was diagnosed with an incurable disease and only has two months to live."

The other man walked into the ring. He also looked nondescript, like he walked in from the same street as the other guy. The exact same street.

"Did I mention they were brothers?" said Gyges.

From their opposite corners, the brothers froze as recognition dawned. A saga played back and forth across the features of their faces as they realized what was before them. To punctuate the dilemma, Gyges made it clear.

"Only one wins," said Gyges. "Or neither."

"This is unconscionable," said the indebted brother.

"Yes," agreed Gyges.

"I can't fight my brother," said the terminal brother.

"Then you'll die," said Gyges as he backed out of the ring.

The brothers faced off. I turned from them. The crowd watched the drama unfold at the center of the ring. But my attention zeroed in on a small corner of the massive arena. Watching the festivities on the other side of the arena in the crowd of thousands, I saw him.

Baros.

13

"*L*oren wait," said Geraint. "Where are you going?"

But Geraint's voice was drowned out. So was the pounding of flesh as one brother took the first swing. I ignored it all as I made my way down the steps towards the ground floor.

My palms sweated as I got nearer to him. My heart was a drum in my ears. The only thing louder was the crack of bones from the arena. I had a fleeting thought, wondering if it was the indebted brother that went down at the terminal brother's hands. Death was a strong motivator, stronger than love.

I'm not sure I believe that; that the fear of death was stronger than the bonds of love. Maybe a few weeks ago, but not now. Especially not when it came to familial love. My shared blood and heritage was a strong pull to do the right thing. Stronger than the man across the way whom I'd shared bodily fluids with.

I wasn't entirely sure what I'd do when I finally reached him. Would I bow to justice and place his hands behind his back and put him under supernatural citizen's arrest? Would I bend to my—*pfft*, not my heart—to my vagina's memories of good times and signal him that the authorities were closing in on him and give him an out?

If I turned him over to the Greeks, he was likely going to finally lie down in the grave he'd avoided for a millennium. Aside from Hades, the Olympians themselves didn't seem overly concerned about his justice. But the Chosen friends of Socrates were out for blood. And rightly so. Baros had participated in the gruesome violation of their friend and nearly brought about Armageddon.

But so had Hera, and no one was going to do anything to her. She was likely off somewhere enjoying the carnal attentions of her brother. That was both unjust and just gross.

Baros had only been an accomplice in the crime. He'd been working toward another goal, trying to gain justice for his people. Yeah, his long dead people who would never reap the fruits of his labors. But his motives weren't totally bad. Were they?

God, where was a moral philosopher when I needed one?

The bottom line was that I had a job to do. I was on a retrieval mission. I was neither judge nor jury. Just the cop coming to pick up the accused.

Wasn't that rich. Me, Loren Van Alst, the po-po. Wait until Baros found out where my alliances lay.

I took him in as I came closer. His pale gaze was fixed on the fighting in the arena. He stood, leaning against a column. His dark curls were shorter than the last time I'd seen him. His tanned arms looked bigger, thicker. They were crossed over his chest and it made his muscles bulge. My steps slowed as my mouth watered.

I wasn't the only one admiring the scenery. There was a crowd of women hanging on him. One trailed her painted nails over his left bicep. Another leaned into his right side, boobs first. But his attention wasn't on any of them. It never was during times like this, when he was preparing to fight.

Love has no place on a battlefield; he'd drilled into my head while I made goo-goo eyes at him. *Steel is the only thing that is dependable. Your blade is your most faithful lover*. Oh, best believe, I made many a dirty joke about that one.

As I crossed to the other end of the arena, the smell of sweat and blood permeated the air. The wet coughs of one of the brothers fighting droned on at the corner of my eardrum. But I was laser focused on that finger running up and down Baros's shirtsleeve.

"I'm going to die, you bastard," said one brother. I assumed the sick one.

"So will I if I don't pay them," said the debtor.

The pounding of flesh and the pleading, familial voices fell away as I came up behind Baros. Damn, had his shoulders always been this big and broad? I spotted that crease at his spine between his shoulder blades. I'd laid the side of my head in that exact spot after he'd worked me over so good that I couldn't get mad when he rolled over to fall asleep.

My gaze was so focused on that spot and the memories it stirred that my tongue was tied. Power and animal magnetism oozed from Baros's pores. It mixed with the blood from the ring and the cries of the crowd and the excitement in the air. I'm woman enough to admit that I got a little lady erection from it all.

"That has to be the biggest sword I've ever seen," said Bimbo Number One.

God, if that wasn't the oldest line in the book. I'd heard it at every swordplay tournament. During those times, before I'd come of age, Baros had gone off with his fair share of the women remarking on his equipment, leaving me on the mat.

I'd already risked my heart for Baros. He'd broken it, time and again. And here I was. At the edge of a ring, inching my way back toward him. I shook myself, and my arousal deflated. Mostly.

"It is a big sword," I said. "Just be aware of its sharp edges."

It was as though a jolt of energy went through Baros's body. He didn't stiffen. He loosened up. He rolled his neck and flexed his fingers. I saw his grin before I saw his opaque eyes. A guttural yell tore through the air from the ring, and I heard the sound of breaking bones. I didn't look over to see which brother was losing.

"Lolo."

"Lenny."

The bimbo whose fingers were wrapped around his bicep wiggled her entire forearm around his arm and then locked in with her other hand. She looked me up and down in a challenge. I reached up and grabbed her by the ear. She squealed like a pink, little piggy as I spun her around and away.

Baros chuckled as the woman teetered away in heels, followed by the other bystander. "You're looking good, Lolo."

"Being alive tends to do that to a girl."

He blinked and his features sobered. A small sigh escaped his lips. "I knew you would get out of that situation back in Greece. I taught you that maneuver and the evasive tactic. If you had failed at it, I would have been very disappointed in you."

So, that's how he was going to play it? Proud teacher to attentive student. I was a grown woman, not a teenager. I knew he was lying. His lips were moving. Not only were they moving, they were forming words through a wolfish grin.

"Really?" I drawled.

My finger trailed to the top button of my shirt. Somehow the button slipped through the hole allowing for a peek at my boobs. Innocently.

My other hand landed on my hipbone. When that happened, I wound up putting most of my weight on one foot and touting my hip, which accentuated the curve of my ass. Precociously.

My brows rose at him. I did a subtle hair flip, to make sure he could see my brow rise. As I did that, my nostrils flared at the musky scent of him, and I licked my lips. Dubiously.

Okay, so I was flirting. Shut up. Have any of you ever seen a Spartan?

No?

Didn't think so. So, don't judge me. Besides, I wasn't seriously showing interest. I was reeling him in and he was playing right into my hand.

Baros reached out and ran his fingers through my hair. My breath came out in a slight shudder as his skin impacted my brow. It's just that it had been a minute since I'd had, well, any loving. So, I might have been just a little off my game. But still, I had this under control.

"I never took you for a nark, Lolo," Baros said.

"Whaa?" Damn it. I couldn't even hold all my consonants together standing toe-to-toe with this man. I tried to recover by inhaling, which inflated my chest. But Baros's gaze wasn't on my breasts. They were focused past me.

"Smells like medieval chivalry," said Baros.

I turned to see Geraint with his brows raised at us. Even with the singeing of Desi's fire from earlier in the day, there was still a phantom of the pointy arch. "Looks like you've found our man, my lady."

"You turning me in, Lolo?"

I turned back to Baros with my finger raised for a point of order. But Geraint got there before I did.

"You're a wanted man, Baros. The Greek Gods have been looking for you."

"If that were true," said Baros, "Zeus would've called me back."

"You came up on our radar in Camelot. Dame Galahad led us to you."

"Dame Galahad?" Baros turned his attention back to me, and finally, I got a chance to speak in between this male sword measuring competition.

"Turns out I'm a descendant of Sir Galahad," I said. "I've been knighted. Can you believe it?"

He smiled at me. It was part pride, part sorrow. "I can't come with you, Lolo. Even if I wanted to. I signed a contract for this tournament. I'm bound by Gyges until I win, lose, or die."

I looked back to the ring as Gyges raised one of the brothers' hands. The man who was left standing was too bloody for me to figure out which one he was. The other—the loser—lay immobile on the ground.

Looking at the scene in the ring, the only thing that ran through my mind were the words Baros' had drilled into my head since I was a kid. *There's no such thing as fairytales. Damsels die. Happiness is a constant, hard-fought battle to be won.*

14

———

"I can't let you sign-up," said Geraint. "You heard what Plato said about Gyges and his sick games. And there are other stories about this guy. Remember the biblical story of King Solomon ordering the two women who claimed they were mothers to one child? He tricked them into revealing their true natures by suggesting they tear the baby in two? Rumor has it that was Gyges's idea. And he wasn't happy when Solomon didn't follow through with splitting the baby into two pieces."

That was pretty sick, but— "I'm not a mom. I don't have any siblings. I can take on any opponent physically, including Baros."

Well, I could hold my own with Baros. I'd never actually won a fight against him.

"It's not just physical, Loren. It's games of morality."

I quirked a brow at Geraint. "You and I both know, despite my oath, that my morals are still pretty loose. It's an advantage."

"What about the psychological impact? Look at what happened to those two human brothers."

The standing brother, the indebted one I'd learned, was off drinking with a bevy of pastel fairies. He didn't look in the least bit haunted at his brother's demise. Though I wondered if he should be taking food from the fae. Weren't there warnings about that?

We'd made our way to the tournament registration table. Surprisingly, there was no one in line. As I took a step toward the table, Geraint tugged at my arm.

"This game is life or death," said Geraint.

"This job, being a knight, is life or death," I said. "Real talk; I'm not sure if I'm ready to turn Baros over. That's the truth."

Geraint blew through his nostrils as his eyes narrowed.

"But," I held up my index finger, "I am certain that no one, including Baros, should have the power of invincibility. That's our true mission; to take the ring out of play."

Geraint's nostrils settled down. He rubbed his forefinger against his hairy chin. I took advantage and stepped up to the table. The bored fairy behind the desk handed me a stack of papers filled with legalese. My eyes skated over the words, which I wasn't sure were in English or any kind of human language. I reached out my hand for the pen the fairy held out.

"Baros is good," I said, palming the fancy fountain pen. "And he's survived this tournament before. He'll likely advance. If I enlist, Gyges would be a fool not to pit us against one another. Imagine that drama; former lovers, student against teacher, man against woman. It screams daytime soap opera."

"And if you lose before you face off against Baros?" asked Geraint.

I snorted. "I won't."

Geraint rolled his eyes.

"The only person who could possibly take me with a sword is Baros ... And you." I quickly added when I saw Geraint's affronted look. I pressed the pen to paper only to see that the well was dry. Before I could even look up to alert the attendant I felt a prick in the padded part of my thumb.

It was like being stuck with a needle. Red ink dripped from the tip of the pen. Looks like the well had been filled with my blood. I wanted to say *ew* and *cool* at the same time. I affixed my signature, with my own blood, and handed the paperwork back to the attendant who took it with a beleaguered sigh.

"If you're signing up," said Geraint, "then so am I."

"You? You're one of the most stoic, rigid, uptight knights there is."

"I think you mean saintly, respectable, and upright." Geraint winced as the pen took its due from his flesh. He affixed his signature to his own stack of papers.

"What I mean is, you'll get crushed in a game of morality."

"You know we took the same oath," he said.

"Yeah," I said. "But you probably said it with an open heart. And no fingers crossed. Kidding."

"They'll probably pit us against each other, like the brothers."

I grinned. "Are you calling me your brother?"

"It's the most logical thing for Gyges to do; to try to make us turn on each other. You should know, I won't go easy on you this time."

We made our way back to the arena just in time for the last bout to end. I didn't see the contenders, only the cleanup crew that mopped up the blood from the ground. In the ring, Gyges was taking center stage again.

"Ladies and gentlefae, we have a treat for you tonight. We've had some late additions to the program. But we'll get this party started early."

Gyges didn't look our way, but I knew he was talking about us. And then, to put a point on it, a blindingly bright spotlight found us in the crowd.

"We are thrilled to have not one, but two knights from the Round Table of Camelot in our presence. Those noble do-gooders have come to battle it out in the arena."

"Told you," said Geraint.

"Up first, coming to you from the lost kingdom of Dumnonia, we have Prince Candor Geraint."

Geraint sighed heavily as the crowd of female fairies tittered, craning their swan necks to get a good look at him.

"Prince?" I said.

Geraint ignored me as he started towards the arena ring. I tripped over my feet to keep up with him.

"As you know, my dear guests, Arthur and his

knights sit at a circular table because they believe everyone is equal. They take vows of chivalry, to show mercy, to never harm a woman."

Poor Gyges was in for a surprise. The oath wasn't that simple. Knights were surrounded by witches, so they knew women to be powerful beings. No knight would ever hurt anyone who was defenseless. But if a witch or a druidess or a drunken sorority sister went on the attack, it was our duty to subdue them as best we could and protect those in harm's way. So, under these circumstances, Geraint was covered.

In light of that news, I posed the most important issue to Geraint. "What kind of prince are we talking about?"

Geraint stepped away from me, but I grabbed onto his shirtsleeve before he could get away.

"I mean, are you like the Windsors who're only a figurehead monarchy? Or are you like Middle Eastern or African princes with an absolute theocracy?"

"Loren!" He snatched his forearm away.

I let him go, holding up my hands in a defenseless motion. True to the rules, he didn't attack me.

"And your opponent ..." said Gyges.

I prepared to make my way into the arena ring, but the spotlight that had lit Geraint darkened, casting me in the shadows. Gyges turned to another corner. I noted it was where he'd been sitting and viewing the festivities. The spotlight shone on a woman sitting next to Gyges's empty seat. The woman winced ever so slightly under the glare of light.

"Enid, my dear," said Gyges.

The crowd gasped. I wasn't sure if it was because of Gyges's choice or because of the exquisite creature his open hand indicated.

You had to be close up to see it, but Enid's throat worked. She unfolded her hands, which had rested primly in her lap, and stood. As she came into the ring it was clear to see that she was absolutely lovely. Her skin was pale lavender, like Gyges's. Her royal blue hair was done up in intricate knots and swirls.

Yeah, I think it was her beauty that made the crowd gasp, not the choice of her as an opponent. Her gaze was hooded allowing me to see her pink eyelids, the same shade of pink as Gyges's. Her demure lips were also the same rosy shade as the man in charge. She looked like the definition and the connotation of femininity brought to life. I smelled a rat.

I tugged at Geraint's shirtsleeve. Then I had to tug again. Just like the crowd, he was mesmerized by

Enid's beauty. "This has to be a moral or psychological trick," I said.

It took him a moment to blink and tear his gaze away from the fairy. "Are you sure?"

"Gyges wants you to think he's pitted you against some defenseless maiden," I said with certainty, looking at the unassuming damsel. "She may look the part, but she's competing for some reason. She wants the ring. Don't fall for the helpless act."

Geraint reached into his bag and pulled out his weapon; a masinko. Our swords were able to hide what they truly were outside of Camelot. My sword took the shape of a folded cane. Geraint's took the shape of the guitar-like musical instrument whose music he loved. He tossed his bag to me and then gave the masinko a shake. His blade took shape, glinting in the stage lighting.

Geraint took his mark. "Please choose your weapon, my lady?"

Enid did not. She stayed still and mute, her eyes cast down. She was a great little actress. But I knew that at any moment she would attack.

Geraint looked at Gyges. The fae had taken his seat back in the special box where Enid had left. He grinned as he watched the festivities play out.

Geraint tossed a look over his shoulder at me. I

gave him an encouraging nod. When he still hesitated, I flicked my fingers at him to get on with it.

He turned back to Enid. She still stared at the floor, not making a single move. It looked like she was barely breathing. I wondered if she was weaving a spell, like a witch?

Geraint took a fighting stance. And held it. I knew he wouldn't strike out first. And so we all waited.

And waited.

And then waited some more.

Finally, Geraint lowered his sword. He turned back to me. But I could only offer him a shrug. I couldn't figure out this chick's game.

Geraint tossed me his sword. He turned back to Enid and took a few tentative steps towards her. I groaned. He was going to lose the battle as chivalry won the day.

But no. Wait. Geraint surprised us all. He came toe to toe with Enid, and then the prince put up his dukes. I pumped my fists in the air. Take that, you psychotic faerie. Gyges wasn't going to pull a fast one on this knight.

Enid chanced a glance up at Geraint. She bit at her lower lip. Geraint's eyes followed the move, but he didn't lower his defense.

A movement below caught my gaze. I saw Enid's fingers twitch. Was she about to reach for something? Was she preparing to do magic? Her slender fingers began to unfurl.

"Geraint, look out," I shouted. "Her hand."

His gaze went down to her hand. Then his own fist struck out. There was a collective gasp from the entire crowd, then silence.

You could hear a pin drop as Enid's head snapped back. Crimson blood rushed under the skin just below her eyes. She blinked twice and then sank to her knees in a puddle of pastels.

All the color drained from Geraint's face as he took her in. A woman sunken down to his feet. Her empty hands went to her bruised face.

Geraint dropped down to her. But she shrank away from him. Enid cowered before him and curled herself into a protective ball.

Maniacal chuckling filled the arena as Gyges made his way back into the ring. "And the winner." Gyges raised Geraint's hand. "Chivalry is dead."

15

"I'm going to hell."

"No," I soothed, rubbing Geraint's back. He was doubled over as we both sat on the lowest rung of the arena seating. "You might qualify for a reality television show, but hell? Nah."

"I've never hit a lady before," he said, straightening. He looked truly forlorn and shaken. "I mean I've battled you, and the Banduri, and an evil witch once. But none of that counts. What woman doesn't know how to defend herself? My God. Listen to what I'm saying. I'm blaming the victim."

Geraint crumpled back into his seat. The people and fairies around us openly stared and pointed at him. It was a knight's worst nightmare—purposefully inflicting pain on an innocent.

I looked back out into the arena as Gyges made his way to the center to announce the next bout. This was truly a sick and twisted game. Even if you won, you lost. And it looked like I was up next.

"Hey, Lolo."

"Hey, Lenny."

Baros held a xiphos in his sword hand. The weapon was the traditional Spartan short sword that had a slightly curved blade. It was mainly used in fighting close combat.

My sword was magical. It could adjust to my needs. Before I knew that it was from the same family as Excalibur, I'd already given it a name. I'd deemed it Inigo for obvious fan of the 80's reasons.

"Nice blade," Baros said.

"Yours, too."

There was no waiting for me to make the first move. Baros was not chivalrous. He raised his sword.

"You're not going to try and talk me out of his fight?" I asked.

He grinned. "I know you too well. You never back down from a fight. Even when you're going to lose. But I promise I'll kiss it better if you come to my rooms after."

I raised my sword. "The only thing that's getting kissed is the handle of my blade by you."

He grinned. "I've always loved your trash talking before a fight."

"I know, both on the mat and on the mattress." And with that, I made the first move.

I came at him with a wrath strike, which he easily parried, taking a step back and exposing his inside. Seeing the opening, I lunged for the unprotected area, extending my sword. Only realizing a second too late that it was a mistake.

The moment my foot lifted to slide forward and sink into the deeper stance for a lunge, Baros raised his own foot ever so slightly. The toe of his boot connected with my instep and sent me off balance. I tucked and rolled, quickly returning to my feet with my sword at the ready.

"Don't lunge," Baros said. He swaggered a few steps around the arena, swinging his sword as he strode. "The second it takes to sink your weight into the longer stance is a second filled with vulnerability."

"Thank you for the tip."

He inclined his head.

I lifted my blade and charged. This time, I sliced down toward his right shoulder. He stepped back with his left foot, and I met air.

I immediately wind-milled my sword arm and

went for his left shoulder. He stepped back with his right foot, and I met the air on the other side of his body. I knew better than to repeat the pattern. The problem was, I was already drawn forward.

It made sense to go for his shoulder again. But when I raised my sword, he was ready for me. I advanced toward his right side. He slipped behind my left shoulder, grabbing my sword arm.

"Don't go where your opponent leads you," Baros growled in my ear.

I inhaled at the feel of his hot breath on the tip of my ear. The feel of his heartbeat pushed the back of my shirt and caressed my spine.

"Lenny? Is that another sword in your pocket? Or are you just happy to see me?"

"Yup."

"Wait," I said. "Which one?"

He gave my back a push. My body tumbled forward, where he'd directed it. His grip stayed on my sword, and he stripped it from my hand.

I looked down at my empty hand. Then at my beautiful blade that was snug in his hold. Hmm? I've never been jealous of steel before, especially when it was my sword.

"Sorry to do this to you, Lolo. You were always my favorite student."

My head jerked up to his face. "Favorite?" I frowned. "You take that back. I was the best. I am the best."

A slow grin spread across his face as he tilted my sword up so that the blade caught the light. Evidence to my lowered stature from best to favorite.

"Oh, that?" I shrugged and flipped my wrists as though to brush off the trivial matter of losing my sword. "That was just a momentary loss of concentration. I was admiring your other weapon."

Baros's grin fell. His lips thinned, and his eyes narrowed. It was his teacher's face. "I taught you better than that. Don't let emotions cloud your judgment."

"I know, I know," I sighed. "No such thing as fairytales. Don't be a damsel. No such thing as love."

"I never said that."

And then the bastard looked at me. You know how men look at you with something that steps outside the boundaries of desire but is a good distance from fondness.

My throat felt dry under his pale gaze. My heart raced. My belly grumbled with upset. "Don't mess with me like that, Lenny."

But his gaze held. His pale eyes softened, as did

his voice. "We'll talk later when you come to my room for that kiss."

"Oh," I chuckled, placing my hands on my knees as I doubled over. "You thought this was over?"

I straightened and opened my hand. Power surged into my palm. I gave a yank and Inigo slipped Baros's grip and returned to me where he belonged.

Baros's eyes widened. A gasp went through the crowd that had been quiet, listening in on this intimate entertainment. There was momentary shock on Baros's face. But then his grin split wide. Battle lust and carnal lust clashed on his features.

"You were holding back on me," he said.

"You were holding back on me," I said. "Did you really think you had me with that little reversal move? Though I totally appreciate the stand to attention."

Baros's grin spread, and he took a fighting stance. He motioned me hither with his long fingers. I managed to stave off the assault of toe-curling memories and took up a fighting stance of my own. And then we charged.

The sound of metal clinking, clashing, slicing, and slashing mixed with the cheers of the crowd. As I tried to run him through with my blade, I couldn't help but admire Lenny's form.

There were many legendary warrior nations. Erikson's Vikings, Kahn's Mongols, and Caesar's legions. But there was nothing like a bare-chested, tree-trunk thighed, well-hung Spartan.

The entire culture was focused around the army. Weakness was not tolerated. Boys entered the military at age seven. Only the men who passed the *agoge* were made full citizens and had rights to land in exchange for military service. War was a Spartan's whole life. There was no militiaman that had other professions. A Spartan warrior's sole responsibility was war and the glory of Sparta.

But Spartans fought as a group, as a unit. I'd only ever fought on my own. The one for all and all for one stuff had only happened to me recently. Baros was used to tight formations and having someone at his flank–like a wingman before there were air pilots. He had weaknesses. And I knew them.

What? Did you seriously think I didn't have a plan? Baros didn't always protect his sides. An opening was coming up right about now. But I decided to take a quick, little detour first.

I advanced, slashing his shirt open and exposing that glorious bronzed work of art. He looked down at the damage I'd done.

"Now, if I did that to you it would be considered sexist," he said.

"I don't make the rules."

I took a moment to admire my handiwork. And then, that was it. I was done playing. I had a job to do, and I was ready to do it. Well, I was ready to win this battle to get to the ring. I wasn't sure if I was ready to lose Lenny to the war.

And then it happened. Baros flicked his wrist. His blade glinted in the arena's spotlight as it advanced on me. But I ducked and rolled out of his reach. He didn't follow me down as he could've. He stayed standing, his blade pointing at me. Mine pointed at him as well.

It looked like a stalemate, but it was so much more. It was a *parry sixte avec riposte*. He'd done it again.

He was looking at me with that soft expression. It was beyond the pride that a teacher had for a student. He looked at me like I was precious. Like I meant something to him.

I came to stand. As I did, my blade pressed into his flesh. His pressed into mine.

"Stop," called Gyges. "Stop."

Without taking our gazes off each other, Baros

and I did as we were told. We lowered our blades, but we did not step away from each other.

"I'm intrigued," said Gyges as he came into the arena. "I want to see this little soap opera continue for the amusement of all. I'm calling a draw. You both advance."

At first, there was silence as we all processed his words. And then there were cheers that rose to the dome of the arena. So loud, I wondered if the tourists milling about above could hear it. When I turned back to the center of the ring, Baros was gone.

16

"Did you see where he went?"

"Did you see where she went?"

Geraint scratched his chin. I scrubbed my fingers through my hair. Then finally, in the silence, where we both were waiting for the other to respond, our gazes connected.

"Who?" I asked.

"Enid," he said. "I saw her in the crowd when your match ended. Who are you talking about?"

"Baros, of course. That's who we're here looking for. Not to try to get you laid."

Geraint's gaze, which had been bouncing around the arena, jerked back to me. "I'm not trying to date her," he said through clenched teeth. "I need to see if she's okay. I wounded her."

"And what? You want to find her to kiss it better?"

"See." He snapped. "There." He pointed his index finger at me. "That wit you think is so cute is as sharp and cutting as your blade."

"I'm sorry." I laid my hand on my breastbone hoping he saw my sincerity. "Let's take a deep breath. We both just faced a part of ourselves that we didn't like or want to see. Emotions are high right now."

We both took deep breaths. Geraint pinched the bridge of his nose and closed his eyes. When he opened them again, he reached out a hand and rubbed me roughly.

"You all right now?" he asked.

"Is that your idea of comfort?" I shrugged off his awkward embrace.

"And the sarcasm is back." He retracted his hand and his affection.

"I use humor as a shield." I reached for his palm and clasped it with mine. "You should know that about me if we're going to be best buddies."

"We're not—"

"I'm sure Enid is fine," I soothed.

Geraint's shoulders slumped. "Someone told me she is Gyges's daughter."

"Seriously?" That was the sickest joke of all.

"Why would he put her in the fight?"

"Remember, you can't enter against your will. There must be something she wants."

"Then why didn't she defend herself to get it?" he asked.

"Maybe Gyges was just using her to get to you? To break you? These games are cruel." And this was only the first round.

"He'll likely put us against each other next. Baros will assume you will ally with him."

Lenny had said to meet him if I lost. I didn't lose. Did that mean the invitation was still open?

"Loren?"

My attention snapped back to Geraint. I was thankful he couldn't see what I'd been thinking. Or could he? The arch was back in his brow.

"Whose side are you on, my lady?" he asked.

"Are you seriously questioning my loyalty?"

"Yes."

"That's fair." I lowered my chin and held my palms up. "But I took the same vows as you. And, honestly, I didn't cross my fingers."

"Love is stronger than vows."

"Ew. I don't love him." My voice sounded like a twelve-year-old girl's who'd just got caught passing a love note. "I lusted after him."

"Lust is an even more powerful motivator," he said. "It clouds the judgment."

"My judgment does get cloudy sometimes," I admitted. "But when the clouds part, the thing that's most important to me is my family. I won't ever let anything bad happen to the people of Camelot. Or Nia. Baros wants freedom. I don't think that's a threat to Camelot."

"Didn't you tell me he tried to bring back a Titan God?"

"Yeah." I elongated the two syllables as I searched for a way to back up my ex. "But it was because he wanted to defeat a Persian immortal. Camelot's in the UK."

Geraint shook his head. "There are witches and squires in Turkey."

"Oh." I bit my lip. "But if Baros does succeed and become free of the Greeks, won't he become just a man again?"

"At one point in history, that man led one of the world's most fearsome armies. Three hundred men lined up behind him to face an impossible situation, knowing death was imminent."

"To protect their families," I insisted. "Doesn't that make him just as good as a knight?"

Confronted with that tidbit, Geraint hesitated.

He was back on his heels. I went in for the kill by pulling on his chivalrous heartstrings.

"I was a thief and a forger before I came to Camelot," I began, ignoring the fact that I had sinned just this morning when I'd forged the invitation into the Olympians' stronghold. "What changed me was having people who believed in me, people who expected more of me. I won't let those people down, and I won't let any harm come to them. Baros is me from a year ago. He lost his family, his brothers, his way. I've changed. I think he has the capacity to do the same."

Geraint pierced me with those eyes. I had an inkling before, but I knew he saw into my soul. The verdict, for me, was good. But Baros didn't fare so well.

"From what I see and hear," said Geraint, "he calls to your baser instincts. What you did during the battle of the Banduri was because of your family that you love and who love you in return. Camelot calls to your best instincts. That's what makes you noble."

I opened my mouth to protest, but then I realized something. "Wait, did you just call me noble? We are so on the road to becoming the best platonic friends in history."

"Baros has no ties to us," said Geraint, ignoring my outpouring.

"He has me," I said. "Well, he doesn't *have* me. But I vouch for him."

Geraint still wasn't trying to hear it. He began turning away from me. I reached out for his arm, but he jerked it from me. Unfortunately, his elbow went wide and into someone's nose. Someone's purple nose.

"Oh no," I groaned.

Geraint turned slowly. Horror registered on his face as Enid sank to the ground clutching her face. She looked up at him with only one eye and that eye was bruised.

"I'm so sorry," he said. "I didn't mean–I didn't know–"

He reached for her, but she scrambled back in her pretty dress, like a crab. Geraint advance on his knees hands up in surrender, voice pleading. "Please, my lady. I never met you any harm. I didn't know you were helpless."

Enid threw up her hands and the prettiest display of sparkles—what you'd imagine a fairy would produce to entertain a child—came out of her dainty hands. A plume of pastel petals swelled just below Geraint's nose. It looked like a tiny mist of pollen. Geraint froze and then began to sneeze.

"I'm a knight," he insisted after another bout of sneezing stopped. "You must know that the thought of harming a woman is my worst nightmare. I thought it was a trick."

He tried to advance again, but vines sprouted up from the ground and wrapped around his limbs. They tugged taut and held him still as Enid came to standing. So, she could defend herself.

Geraint continued to struggle, determined to get his apology out. He broke through a few vines with his arm. When he did, thorns grew out of the vines, their prickers sharp and clawing into his flesh.

Finally, he held still. "All right. I deserve this. And worse. But if ever you need it, for the rest of my days, my sword is at your command."

Enid stared down at him. A flicker of—something—sparked in her eyes. But then her gaze shuttered, dying like the embers of a snuffed fire. She backed away from him and, without another word, ran away into the crowd.

17

I left Geraint in the infirmary in the care of a light pink fairy. She laid her shimmering hands on him, and his wounds began to close before our eyes. But the fairy healer's eyes stayed fixed on Geraint's lips and not on the scratches and gouges in his flesh. For his part, Geraint's attentions remained focused out on the entryway. Though I doubted Enid would make another appearance anytime soon.

I had a bruise of my own forming from my fight with Baros, but I didn't want to sit in the infirmary and fight for the healer's attention. Besides, it wasn't her hands I was interested in. I knew what would solve my aches and pains, and so I headed in the direction of the lodgings that had been set up for those staying in the arena for the night.

I hadn't told the entire truth in my debate on ethics with Geraint. The whole truth was I didn't believe people could change. Not really. You could make different choices from time to time. But the person you were born as was the person you remained.

Look at me. I was a prime candidate. I'd taken vows to be a chivalrous servant of the innocent, but here I was, once again, taking a walk on the dark side. I stepped down the dark stone steps marveling at the shape that this sub-level of the magical arena was in.

Where the Colosseum, the above structure that was visible to the human eye, was crumbling and dilapidated, what lay beneath the surface was filled with luxury from the stone walls to the glossy floors. Along with my registration pack, I'd been handed a hotel-styled key card. I passed by the room that had been assigned to me and headed farther down the narrow corridor.

My movements were a choice, a decision that I made before the fight between myself and Baros had been won—or tied as it were. Geraint had it right; Baros did call to my baser instincts. But just because they were the baser ones and not the high and lofty ones, didn't make them wrong. It didn't make me evil that I was choosing this walk on the dark side. Hell, sometimes it was just more fun in the shadows than it was in the light.

Besides, I was just popping over for a visit on the dark side. I wasn't going to stay there. A lot of society got up to go to work during the day. They were responsible while the sun came up. But when night fell, they wanted to let their hair down at the bar or the club. No one stayed at the club into the new day.

Okay, maybe I had once or twice, but we're getting away from my point.

I might like a little darkness every once in a while, but I'd never allow any shade to touch my family. The thing was, Baros had once been my family. He'd held me after my father had died. He'd been the person I'd turn to to make me strong.

Sure, he wasn't always there for me. And, yes, sometimes he was occupied with some floozy in his arms. But when he actually gave me his attention, I felt important.

There was good in him. And I had even more evidence now. He hadn't killed me back in Greece, and he hadn't killed me tonight in Rome. That had to count for something.

Stepping up to Baros's door, I took a moment to check the flyaways of my hair and straighten my clothes. I was only here to talk, but I wanted to look good, of course. What woman wouldn't want to look her best when she was going to see her ex, late at night, just to talk?

From the moans and groans coming from behind Baros's door, it sounded like some other booty had beat me to the call. No, wait, make that a couple of booties. From the squeals and giggles, it sounded like Baros had a late night celebration going on.

Had he forgotten he'd told me to stop by?

Maybe I'd taken too long, and he'd thought I'd forgotten?

Or maybe he thought I'd stood him up?

Wait a minute. What the hell was I thinking? Was I making excuses for him?

God, I was an idiot. Had I seriously thought that I could save this man? Baros was Darth Vader to the core. I was gonna hand him his ass tomorrow in the tournament, and then hand him back to the Olympians myself.

I balled my hands into fists and turned on my heel. Stalking back down the hall, I saw that Geraint's door was closed and the light spilled out from the small space at the bottom. I didn't want to face him and see his brow arch with an *I told you so.* So, I headed into my room.

It took the key card three tries before it worked. So, this underground fairyland wasn't immune from the traps of malfunctioning technology. I flipped the switch for the lights and froze in the doorway.

Baros sat on the edge of the bed. His elbows were on the knees of his man-spread thighs. I'd avoided Geraint because I didn't want to hear him say I told you so. But it looked like I wasn't escaping that phrase tonight. I told you so was clearly written on Baros's face.

"What are you doing here?" I demanded.

"Came to tend your wounds like I promised."

"I'm not hurting." The door slipped from my hands and closed with a quiet snick. "Besides, shouldn't you be at your party?"

"I'm exactly where I want to be." His pale eyes smoldered as he stood, straightening all six-foot-plus of his muscled bulk.

"You did that on purpose. You invited those girls into your room because you knew I'd go there."

In just two steps, he had his large body pressed against mine. He slammed my back against the door and leaned into my ear. His breath was a hot caress as he spoke.

"I came here," he said. "Isn't that what matters?"

"You're still an asshole."

"Of course," he grinned. "People don't change, Lolo. You know that. You know me. The good parts. The bad parts. The dirty parts. You know exactly what you're going to get."

It took everything in me not to tilt my head up. I knew that if I did, I'd be lost in his vacant gaze like always. Somehow, I managed to step around him. "Well, I've changed."

His hand snaked out and grabbed my forearm bringing me back to him. The rough handling stole my breath and made my mouth water. I liked it a little rough, and he knew it.

"You've acquired new allies and new skills since last time we were together," Baros said. "But you're the same. Same curiosity in that little head. Same fire on that silky tongue. Same sense of adventure in your heart. But something new, also. I can smell the power, the energy, coming off you."

Baros pulled me closer, his hold was absolute. He brought his nose near my temple and inhaled. It felt like his breath pulled the answers from deep inside me. I felt a tingling sensation from my toes all the way to my belly.

When he'd found the scent he wanted, he pulled

away, just a fraction, and smiled down at me. "I always knew you were special, but a witch?"

It dawned on me then. "Is that why you want me now? Because I'm a witch."

"I've always wanted you. Even before it was proper. Whether it be to train you, to guide you, to mold you, to touch you. I knew you'd be the key to my future happiness."

He was BSing me. I knew it as a fact because his mouth was moving. The words that were coming out were so pretty it could be nothing but lies.

His large hand slid down my spine. I clenched my teeth to keep from shuddering. From revulsion, of course.

"Let me go," I said.

"No."

The hand that he used to hold my wrists firm made its way to my temple. He gently moved a flyaway from my brow and twirled it around his fingers.

My hands that had been captive just stayed there, suspended in the air. I couldn't move them or my feet. Baros never needed physical control over me to bend me to his will. My muscles felt like they were spasming as I warred with making them move away and wanting to move closer. In the end, I split the difference and decided to play with fire.

Baros released his other hand from its loose hold on my back as the magical fire blazed between us. He stared, transfixed at the flame in my palm. It was my best trick, so of course, I brought it out for show and tell.

I didn't know if I was trying to scare him away or impress him. In the end, I'm not sure it did either. He stepped into my hand, right into the burning flame.

I went to pull back, but he held my wrists. The blaze consumed the cotton of his shirt. Baros only winced at the obvious pain.

I was stunned. I had no choice but to extinguish the fire. But something had already reignited between us.

I reached up and pulled his head down to mine. He came willingly, licking into my mouth like a match searching for the flame. My hands landed on his bare chest. His skin felt hotter than the magic still burning in my fingertips.

We were burning up together. But at the same time, I felt bathed in the coolness of familiarity. Baros bit the edge of my lip, sinking in his incisors until I tasted the tint of blood. I bit back, of course.

His large hand cupped the back of my head. I

was only able to take a short gasp of breath before his fingers bunched into a fist, and he gave my tresses a firm yank. I groaned as my head was jerked back and the column of my neck exposed.

"There's my good girl," Baros crooned.

I wanted to rail. I wanted to yank out of his grasp and launch a protest. I was not his. I was not a girl anymore. But damn, it was good.

And so I let him run his teeth along the sensitive spot at the pulse point beneath my jaw. I let him yank open my shirt, the buttons spilling to the floor. I let him toss me onto the bed like I was a rag doll and pull off my pants. I let him tear off his own pants and listened intently as he detailed all the naughty and depraved things he was about to do to me.

But I didn't let him mount me. I did have some pride, after all. The moment he tried to straddle me, I flipped him over onto his back, reversing our positions like a cowgirl would hop into her saddle. Then I held him down and rode him like we were on borrowed time and running from the law.

18

Ah man, was I sore. My cramps and twinges and knots were greater in number and spread wider over my body than when Baros and I had faced off in the ring. But we'd used more weapons than swords in the bed. There had been hands and mouths and teeth and even feet.

I'd worn him like a pair of shoes that had to be returned before the stroke of midnight. In return, he'd cracked my back. You know what I mean when I say cracked my back, right? When it's so good your spine jackknifes off the bed and bends backward like that girl in *The Exorcist*.

Oh, yeah. The aftershocks were still rumbling in my core. My pinkie toes still hadn't uncurled. My lower back wasn't quite touching the mattress yet.

Baros lay next to me, propped up on his elbow, looking down and admiring his handiwork. With his forefinger, he traced the bite marks he'd made on my breasts. His finger played a game of Connect the Dots as he went on down to the handprints he'd left on my hips. That particular mark was a masterpiece; the palm print of his hand was on my hipbone. The mark ended with the indents of his fingerprints on my ass.

I squirmed, getting hot and bothered again just thinking about the things we'd been doing for hours. Yes, hours. Because a Spartan warrior could go all night and into the dawn.

It wasn't dawn yet. I knew that because I still had a few bars of service on my cell phone even though we were deep underground and away from satellites and cell towers. But hey, there was also a dragon and fairies running around down here, so who was I to question that the world above could hear me now if I made a call.

Anyway, I took a deep breath and snuggled into the bedding. I tried urging my lower back farther down into the mattress, but it was still arched with pleasure. Baros could tell. I saw it in his smug grin. I doubted I could go another round with him without passing out or breaking some tender part of my body. Besides, I was vulnerable enough already, and I was certain our time together was just about up.

Baros loved sex, but he didn't like to sleep in the same bed with his lovers. He was gentlemanly enough to cuddle after. In the past, he'd usually waited until I'd fallen asleep to make his getaway. He didn't know it was worse when I woke up in an empty bed. I'd much rather he walked out while I was still awake. He looked comfortable lying in my bed as he traced my skin like he was in no hurry to leave.

"Dame Galahad?" he said.

"What of it?" I said.

"Those knights let you near their treasures?"

"Actually, no." I picked at an imaginary piece of lint on the pillow between us. "I'm still on a bit of a probationary status due to some ... misunderstandings."

Baros laughed. At one point in my life, it had been my sole mission to make this man laugh. His chuckle was a deep, rolling baritone that I felt in the pit of my belly. With my stomach exposed to him now, I felt it lower, and I had to press my thighs together.

"Misunderstandings? What did you do?"

I shrugged. "I may have rushed blindly into a

battle, caused an invasion of Camelot, and nearly gotten an innocent killed. You know, the normal bit."

"That's my girl."

I tensed. My thighs loosened their squeezing and, instead, I crossed my legs at the knees. My toes finally uncurled as numbness settled in. The small of my back landed with an anticlimactic thud on the mattress.

I wasn't his girl. I was working here. This little interlude was just a perk of the job.

I felt no shame. Men played women all the time in spy movies. Now, I was turning the tables. Equal rights. Right?

"I missed you, Lolo."

My fingers, which had been picking at the pillow fabric, went slack. I looked away from him, careful to avoid those lusterless eyes whose depths were so easy to get caught in. I blinked a couple of times, trying to regain my Bond-like focus and stick to the mission at hand. But my quivering lady parts still held the mic.

"If that were true, you would've come found me after Greece."

Baros shook his head. "You were with your new friend, Dr. Rivers. She would've turned me over to the Olympians."

He had a point. Nia would've handed his ass over to the Olympians and held him still while he paid for his crime against her friend, Socrates. Did he think I would've stood by her while that happened? At the time, I was pissed enough that he would've been right. But now …?

I turned over, facing him, but not looking him in the eye. I focused on his broad chest, planting a trail of kisses there to distract him from his prior line of thinking. I nearly got off track myself. That man's body was a wonderland of planes and ridges and bulges.

"So, what's the plan?" I asked. "Double-cross everyone and get the ring for ourselves?"

He chuckled and, now that my legs were no longer pressed together, the deep rumble hit me right between the thighs. He tilted my head up and captured my lips. I let him. It was such hard work, my job.

"Only one person can hold the ring," he said when he let me up for air.

As he spoke, he rotated the ring on his finger. I remembered that ring. He hadn't worn it when I'd known him before. But when we were reunited back in Budapest, he'd had it. Nia had noticed it too.

Both my bestie and I had grabby hands when it

came to ancient artifacts. She'd been focused on the ring, while my attention had been on its bearer. All that I knew about the ring was that it was as old as Baros, likely from his time.

"If you want to hold the Ring of Gyges," Baros continued, "it will exact a hefty price. It will take what you hold dear to give you what you dream."

"You're holding me a little dearly right now," I said.

His gaze broke from his hand and focused on me. That had been a miscalculation on my part. I gulped as he caught me with those pale eyes.

"You won't take possession of the ring," he said. "You have no need for it."

"You have no idea what I dream of."

"Yes," he nodded, wrapping his arms tightly around me. "I do. You already have it."

Cocky bastard.

"Once I have my freedom from the Olympians, there will be no reason we can't be together."

My head tilted as though the heavy doubt would pop my top off. I cocked my head away from him, but I didn't get far. He leaned in, preparing to capture my lips. I had no escape. I'd have to take the onslaught of his affection.

But at the last second, he pulled away. "Unless there's someone else? A knight perhaps?"

"Who?" I asked half dazed, half confused. "Geraint? No. I am so not his type. He doesn't even like me—yet. Well, he does like me. He's just fighting our budding bromance."

"Then there's nothing standing in our way."

When I didn't answer him immediately, Baros's empty gaze narrowed. "Unless you want to remain at the Round Table?"

"It does have its perks," I admitted. "Three square meals a day for one. But I'll never get fat with the knight's daily training program. And there's plenty of leisure time during the evenings to visit with others."

"You just described a daily prison routine," said Baros.

I shoved away from him. It wasn't a prison. It was the family I'd lost and found. They always stuck by each other. They never crawled out of bed before sunlight.

Baros chuckled again. I pressed my thighs together just in time. Still, the sound waves of his laugh got under my skin. It put me off balance, and Baros pulled me closer.

He reached down and grabbed the comforter,

wrapping it around both of our naked bodies. He placed a tender kiss on my temple, which rocked me. Baros didn't do tender, at least not with me. Unless he wanted something.

"Are you ready for another round?" I asked.

"No, woman. You've worn me out. But definitely in the morning."

"You mean when you come back in the morning? After you go to your bed to sleep?"

"Why would I leave a warm, sated woman?" He snuggled down into the mattress and tucked his head between my neck and shoulder.

My tongue-tied. I couldn't figure out a response to that one. It didn't matter. By the time I inhaled to gather words, he was snoring softly. It didn't look like he was about to go anywhere anytime soon.

19

———

$\mathcal{I}$t wasn't the knock on my door that jolted me awake. It was the strong arms that held me locked down in the bed. It was the warm front that was pressed into my back that shook me.

What the hell? Who the hell? He was still here?

I reached out to the bed stand and tapped the face of my phone. It was eight in the morning. The movement of my body placed an inch of air between us. Baros gave a tug and pulled my torso back to him in what felt like a protective gesture.

The person on the other side of the door knocked again. This time it was more of a pound, like the way the police would knock when they had a warrant. Baros raised his head. His entire body tensed. I felt his sword hand itch as it gripped my hip.

"Loren," called Geraint. "Get up. This isn't a vacation. We have work to do."

So, it was the authorities after all. But that particular branch of authority was here for me and not Baros. I made to move but then realized that one, there was a tether to my body, and two, my body was naked. I couldn't answer the door to my brother-at-arms while naked with a fugitive latched onto my hip.

The pounding on the door stopped. But then the door handle rattled. Thank God it was locked. Otherwise, Geraint would've gotten an eyeful of a Baros and Loren pretzel, the salty variety after all the sweat from our amorous activities. That would not look good on my job performance report. God, what if he actually was going to do a performance report?

"Just a minute," I croaked, rolling out of bed.

"Hurry up," said Geraint. There was a thunk on the door, which I assumed was his big body leaning into the frame.

Baros growled at the door. I was so stunned my voice stuck in my throat. Yeah, me. The girl who was never at a loss for words.

Baros had never done that before. He'd never

appeared to care when another man showed interest in me. Not that Geraint was showing interest in me. But Baros didn't know that.

"Loren?" Geraint packed so much into the two syllables of my name. There was suspicion and disappointment and inevitability.

Well, it didn't look like I'd be able to slip out of the door without Geraint getting a look inside. Or that I'd be able to shove Baros in the closet so that Geraint wouldn't see him. It looked like these two men were about to come face-to-face.

It was time to put on my big girl panties. Wait? Where exactly were my panties?

I searched around on the floor, but only found my pants. I dove for them. While I was putting in the second leg I noticed that the Baros-shape that had been in the bed had vanished. I blinked, looking left and then right. To my horror, I saw him making his way to the closed door.

I had just enough time to pull up my pants. It would be a commando kinda day. I didn't have time to pull on my bra. I'd just managed to get my head in my shirt when Baros yanked the door opened.

The light from the hall illuminated the room, my half-dressed state, and Baros's full frontal nudity. I have never let a man fight my battles, but damn if

Baros's possessive swagger as he blocked Geraint's path wasn't sexy. Unfortunately, I had to cut short my admiration. I yanked down my shirt to cover my hipbone, but not before giving Geraint a glance at my bare who-ha first.

"You're the knight." Baros looked Geraint up and down.

"You're the Spartan." Geraint looked Baros up, but as his eyes drifted down, he groaned and looked away as though he'd been blinded. His gaze landed on me.

"Hey, Gee." I waved. "What up, bruh?"

"My lady," said Geraint. His eyebrow working overtime as he took in me, the room, and the bed.

"She's not your lady," growled Baros. "Bruh."

Geraint's brow crinkled with distaste. "I'm not your bruh, but her—" He gave the door a shove and Baros lost his hold, making way for Geraint to enter. "She's a sworn knight of the Round Table, and a witch, which makes her family.

"Aw, Gee," I said. But was immediately silenced by his unwavering brow of disapproval. He looked down at my groin area. I followed his gaze to see that I was still unbuttoned. I turned around and handled my business.

"Family?" said Baros as he let the door close with

a snick, but he still didn't bother to reach for any clothing. "You don't have the porcelain features of a Saxon. Where are your people from?"

Geraint looked between the two of us before answering. "My mother was Saxon. My father was from Al-Maghreb. That's present-day Morocco."

"You're not Persian?"

"I'm a Moor."

Baros relaxed now that he knew that Geraint wasn't Persian. He swaggered over to me, still naked as the day he was born and completely unconcerned about his junk hanging out. He came to stand behind me, wrapping his arms around me from the back.

I stiffened in his embrace. He never showed PDA. Like ever.

"Um, Lenny? Do you mind if I talk to my brother here alone?"

Baros looked from me to Geraint, then back to me. Without warning, he dipped my head back and planted a possessive kiss on my lips. His hand on my neck screamed ownership. His tongue in my mouth marked me as his territory.

"I'll see you in the arena," he whispered, his pale eyes locked on mine in conspiracy. "For the win."

He straightened my spine and let me go. In all

honesty, I wobbled when I was left to my own two feet. I watched, stunned, as he pulled on his clothes and then headed for the door. But he paused again in front of Geraint.

"May you reach the limits of virtue before you cross the border of death."

"Um...?" Geraint looked to me for some direction, but I had none. He turned back to Baros. "All men make mistakes, but a good man yields when he knows his course is wrong and repairs the evil."

Baros grinned. "That was from Sophocles."

Geraint nodded.

"I knew the man. He was a bastard."

And with that, Baros winked at me and then left out the door.

"You know seduction isn't a part of the job description," said Geraint once the door was closed.

"That was closure." I waved his concern away even as the thumping of my heart betrayed me. But Geraint couldn't hear that. "Now, I'm back on the clock."

"I've known guys like him. Gawain used to be him. It took a date with death to get him to clean up his act. Baros's intentions with you are not honorable."

So what? It wasn't like my intentions were honorable with him. I had just been using him. Even though I didn't actually get anything out of him. Except for a couple of mind-blowing orgasms and a cramp in my leg.

"I meant what I said, Loren. You can call yourself a witch or a knight or a woman. Whichever you choose, you are family, and I won't allow someone to dally with you."

Oh, great. Now I was gonna get the overprotective treatment that Morgan hated. It was going to be tedious having these men watch my every move into and out of bedrooms.

I ran into Geraint's chest and wrapped my arms around his stiff torso. He gave a huge and hefty sigh. Slowly, the stiffness seeped out of his spine. Then he patted me on my back, awkwardly.

Just weeks ago, this man had turned his nose up at me. Look at us now. It made a girl think; maybe people could actually change.

"I think maybe he's changed," I said into Geraint's chest. I knew I didn't need to clarify the who I was talking about.

"Loren," Geraint sighed. "You are not *that* girl."

I pulled out of his embrace with a huff. "You're just jelly I got some last night. Meanwhile, you were pulling thorns out of your ass."

"Loren."

I actually stomped my foot and balled my fists. "He's different."

Geraint shook his head. "That's you. You're different. You're seeing him differently."

"I kinda like what I see."

"Only kinda?" asked Geraint. "Let me guess, what you're feeling, you don't trust it completely. You don't trust that this new attitude of his will stick."

"No," I admitted grudgingly. "But I like it."

"You deserve a guy who will stick."

"I could make a sticky fingers joke here because, you know, former thief and bad girl."

Geraint shook his head again. "You were born a noble lady. It's just that no one told you. When you found out who you were, you stepped up to your destiny."

I flopped down on the bed and my underwear popped out from under the pillow Baros had been laying on. "Why are you giving me the locker room pep talk, coach? You don't even like me."

"You've worn me down." Geraint huffed, looking truly exhausted. Then he looked at me with those dark eyes that I was certain saw more than he let on. "He's going to hurt you, you know."

"Yeah, I know," I sighed.

"I hate to even ask, but you know I have to. We're still on the same team, right?"

I glared at Geraint, but then I let out a tired sigh. I'd barely gotten any sleep, but I was wide awake and alert. "Baros has cheated on me, left me broken-hearted, nearly tried to kill me twice. It's a no-brainer."

I may have been wide awake, but with all that was coming at me, my problem was that my brain was fried. I was still standing in the middle of the field. I wasn't sure which team I belonged on.

20

The pyro display in the middle of the arena would make a rock band look like an afternoon tea party and cause a WWE wrestler to wet his spandex. It was the Fourth of July underground, but it looked like the fireworks display went up into the sky. I knew it was all magic, but it looked real.

I took a moment to enjoy it like I was a spectator. I'd even snapped a couple of pictures of the festivities and sent them to Nia. But she hadn't responded.

I kept looking around, expecting to see her storm in. This was right up her alley, after all. Supernatural shenanigans with an ancient artifact as the prize. She must've been underneath one of her paramours, or if she'd learned anything from me, both of them.

I put my phone away when Gyges preened onto center stage. Today's costume was even more flamboyant than the previous night. He was in a neon yellow that rivaled the brightness of the sun. I wasn't the only one shading my eyes from offense at his fashion sense.

"This is the main event." Gyges's voice reverberated in the air as another blast of sparkly illuminations lit up the fake sky. The words 'main' and 'event' materialized in a number of languages and bounced off the walls of the arena. The crowd went wild even though nothing had happened yet. You could feel their bloodlust as they squirmed in their seats.

There were five contestants still standing. The indebted brother who'd prematurely ended the life of his ailing brother. A second man, whose fight I had not paid attention to. Then there was me and Geraint and Baros. We all stood in a loose cluster; not too close to each other that we were within striking distance.

Gyges focused his attention on us. His purple skin positively glowed with excitement. His pink lips were painted orange today, but somehow it worked with his yellow ensemble. "This is the final battle, my little urchins. Today, one of these five will achieve the quest for invincibility."

The crowd erupted into more cheers. As the fairies in the audience pumped their arms and flapped their petal-like wings, more sparkles filled the air. It was a bit hard to breathe with all the fairy dust clogging the air like aerosol making its way to the ozone.

Gyges raised his hands and the crowd instantly settled. "As you know, the ring will only choose one wearer. Now comes the test of the words *alliance, friend, lover, family.*"

He smiled at each of us in turn, his gaze lingering the longest on me. His smile curled up cruelly, reminding me of the Grinch as he went about his holiday thievery.

"What would you do for the power of invincibility?" he said to the crowd.

In the crowd, people turned to each other. Gazes narrowed shrewdly as they looked sideways at companions or avoided eye contact completely. Bodies shifted closer to some and away from others. Gyges seemed to have a way to bring the worst out of people.

"Luckily for us, we don't have to decide," said Gyges. "We get to watch the entertainment along with our loved ones."

And just like that, the tension eased and light

laughter spread through the arena. Gyges backed up, not looking where he was going, he found his seat. To his left was Enid.

Enid sat stoically in soft pastels. Her head was downcast, her face carefully expressionless. The bruises that had shaded her eyes and her nose from Geraint's ill-timed attentions were gone.

I felt Geraint tense beside me, that's how I knew he'd spotted her too. His lips were parted, but at the same time, his jaw was clenched. He took a step forward. Only one. It could've been taken as a change in stance, but if you knew his character, you'd know that chivalry was puffing up his chest and fogging his brain.

I gave him a shake of my head to try and hold him at bay. But it wasn't my warning that he heeded.

In my peripheral vision, I caught Enid give an almost imperceptible shake of her head. Her eyes didn't leave the floor; her facial expression didn't change. The only way I could be sure of what I thought I'd seen was the barest breath of golden dust that shimmied off her shoulders from the movement.

The crowd didn't notice, but someone else did. Gyges's grin widened at the display of his daughter and his contender. How would he use that against

Geraint? Or maybe it had already worked. Geraint was off his game with his concern for Enid before the game had even started.

I turned my ire towards Enid, but with a glance, I knew she took no pleasure or part in her father's sport. Whatever she was to Gyges, she was not happy. I knew the look of a person happy in their family. I especially knew the look of a daughter sitting in the presence of a father who loved her. The two fairies did not paint that picture.

"The rules are," Gyges was saying. But then he paused dramatically, turning his face up to the crowd. "You know how that phrase ends."

"There are no rules." The shout came from the entire crowd, save the five contestants.

"Just know that once you get to the ring, the battle is far from over." Gyges raised his hands and a set of doors opened.

We all took steps into the opening, all in a straight, wide line. No one in front of or behind the other. Behind us and in front of us were five large eyes. I looked over my shoulder to see my face on the biggest HD screen of my life. The squires and knights would've salivated over such a retinal display.

Seeing all the contenders on the screen, I

supposed each of the eyes were cameras. There were also shells floating next to the cameras picking up the sound of our feet crunching over loose gravel and our bated breaths.

The doors shut with a resounding thud. There was no escape. The only way through was forward.

Out before us, was a maze with many paths to choose from. There was a manicured road that looked well kept. The grass was trimmed back from the path. Along the edges of the path, it was lined with roses. This, I supposed, was the easy road.

A second path was muddy. I could even smell a stench wafting in the breeze from that way. It looked like it would be hard work to navigate that particular path.

The final path, the one at the far end of the maze, was a broken road. It looked treacherous with fragmented cobblestones that begged for a sturdy ankle to turn. That way looked like it would take more than hard work. It looked like it would take your life if you chose its path.

As the men set about pondering which road to choose, I immediately knew the answer. I turned around. To my left stood Baros, to my right stood Geraint. I tugged my lower lip into my mouth as I tried to remember whose side I was actually on and whose side I was pretending to be on. Before I rallied with an answer, I heard a gasp and then a thud.

Cheers rose up from behind the closed door as the crowd went wild. Something told me not to turn, but my back was to the danger, so I had no choice. Sure enough, I turned to find that the indebted brother had gutted the fifth contender. The man withdrew his blade and now it was aimed at me.

There was an intrigued gasp and a few boos from the peanut gallery that sat safely on the other side of the door. That was kinda cool. I'd become a crowd favorite.

Before I could lift a finger to defend myself, a dagger flew into the two-faced brother. The hilt of the dagger protruded from his chest. It was a kopis blade, the type of blade issued to a Spartan warrior. The next cheers I heard were decidedly feminine. I guess Baros and I got some points with the unrequited love story angle.

The indebted brother looked down at his chest in stunned silence. With a gasp of his own, his body fell to the ground with a loud thud. I felt no love loss for the brother as he lay still on the ground.

When I turned to thank my savior, I saw that I

stood in the middle of a third standoff. Both Baros and Geraint had their blades raised, and they were pointed at each other. The next gasp that rose in the air was mine.

"Step aside, my lady," said Geraint. One of the camera eyes floated around his curved scimitar to capture the action as it pointed at Baros.

"The lady can fight her own battles," said Baros. His own blade, a broad xiphos, would've met Geraint's blade if I hadn't been standing between them. "And she knows exactly where she wants to stand."

Part of me wanted to let them fight it out. They were evenly matched. I could let them destroy each other and not let them know where I'd decided to stand.

Problem was, I had a vagina and not a pair of balls. And I'd put on a pair of panties before coming to do battle, the big girl variety. So, I had to face this like a woman.

"You knights are an honorable lot," sighed Baros. "You would've made good Spartan soldiers. It's a shame you have to die."

"The Spartans were a noble breed." Geraint nodded, not taking his eyes off Baros's blade. "It's a shame your kind will now be extinct."

So, this was happening right now. I'd have to take my side. Man, why couldn't I have them both? My old flame and my new brother.

It would be like a reverse harem. Except I didn't want to sleep with Geraint. He'd really become like my brother these past two days. I had not a single naughty thought about him.

Oh, I'd had some when I'd first met him. But then he'd opened his mouth and lifted his brow. Now I got all warm and fuzzy when I thought about him like I did when I thought of Zane, Nia's ex ... or maybe he was her current lover. I really needed to catch up with my bestie and trade notes. Whatever was going on with her couldn't top my cray-cray right now.

"Loren!"

"What?" I looked up to see which man had called my name. It had been both of them.

"Games up, my lady," said Geraint. "I'll take it from here. Move out of the way."

I frowned over at Geraint. Was he seriously pulling this macho BS right now? The word fascist was on the tip of my lip as I channeled Morgan. I could totally take care of myself. How many times did I need to prove that?

"Lolo," crooned Baros. "This is just like we planned. Once he's out of the way, it'll be down to the two of us. I'll have my freedom with the ring, and then we'll be together."

My brow wrinkled at Baros. Why did he keep insisting that he was the prize worth having? He was the one who'd taught me that monogamy was a fool's errand, but all of a sudden, now, he was shoving the committed life in my face.

And then there was Gyges. I could feel him snickering at my predicament as I stood between my past and my present trying to determine the course of my future. But that demented fairy didn't know who he was messing with.

"Wait," I said, holding out my hands to both men. "This is my responsibility. Let me take care of it."

I took a deep breath and turned to Baros. I took a

step toward him. Then I gave him my back and faced Geraint.

Geraint's eyes narrowed at me and then widened as my hand ignited in witch fire. I almost smiled. My harshest critic finally thought better of me. Damn, if it wasn't a hard-won battle and just in time. I saw Baros's triumphant grin reflected in Geraint's wide gaze.

"You told me yourself," I said to Geraint. "People don't change." I spread my enflamed fingers in the shape of a V, better known as the greeting of a Vulcan.

Geraint groaned, lowering his sword and tipping his head back to look up at the fake sky. "Damn it, Loren. Really?"

"Sorry, bruh. But you asked for it."

He let out a long exhale and something that sounded like a muttered curse, or a mumbled prayer, before he re-fixed his gaze on me. "You will pay for this. You know that right?"

I didn't doubt it. "I'm a thief. I don't pay for anything."

Power surged through me, collecting in the palm of my hand. I flicked my wrist, shooting the energy outward; concentrating hard to make sure that this time I hit my mark.

Geraint went down in the third loud thud of the evening's festivities. His eyes shut, and his mouth went slack. Luckily, he didn't convulse in a fit of tickles like Maurice. Geraint lay still as a stone.

For a second, I wondered if I'd actually killed him. But I still felt the hum of the magic from his witch ancestry. I hoped he wasn't out for too long.

It was time for me to turn around and face the man I'd picked for the record. But there was a scratch as my body went into motion, and I realized I might have chosen wrong. Baros's sword was still raised. Was this gonna be a two-sided double-cross?

But he lowered his sword and reached his hand out to me. I stared at the offering for a long moment, not quite sure how this worked. I slipped my fingers between his.

The next thing I knew, I was holding Leonidas Baros's hand, in public. We'd never entwined anything that wasn't naughty before. It was kinda weird and incredibly intimate. Especially since we were doing it in front of a crowd. But when in Rome, right?

I stepped over Geraint's body and allowed Baros to lead me towards the path.

"Which path?" he asked.

I told him what I'd figured out the moment we

entered this maze. "The path we travel doesn't matter. It's the decisions we make along the way."

Igraine's words came through. I'd known they would. I just hadn't known when or how. Man, if I could get her to pay attention to the lottery, all of Camelot would be set until the end of time.

Baros gave me a tug toward the easy path; the one filled with flowers. We strolled along and it felt like we were in a romance movie montage. My hand in his felt warm ... and sweaty. My hand, not his.

It wasn't just my palms and the spaces between our hands that were perspiring, my armpits felt like two small rain clouds had settled there. My slippery fingers didn't seem to bother Baros. He just held on tighter. And then he leaned in and kissed me on my temple like we were some normal couple out on a stroll.

What the hell was going on? This couldn't be happening. Not to me. I wasn't this girl. The girl in the fairy-book or romance novel who got the guy. The girl in high school who met her first and only love, or the one who married her college sweetheart. And definitely not the girl who, after heartbreak after heartbreak, picked the right guy who finally stuck by her.

I kept sweating buckets as the possibility settled

on me like a freight train. Was Baros choosing me? Was I actually walking into some kinda happily-ever-after?

Did I want to?

With him?

He was the first guy who'd ever gotten my heart to skip a beat. Yeah, okay, there were some dead and unconscious bodies in our wake. But he was holding my hand. We were marching down a field of freaking flowers.

Was this fate? If so, then why was my skin itching?

My heart was pounding in my ears. My feet stumbled on a nonexistent rock in our path. Baros caught me and set me back on my feet. I looked into his pale eyes and the earth moved.

No, wait. The ground actually shook. Like it was an earthquake. Because it was an earthquake. The ground around us was splitting and showing its insides and breaking up this idyllic ending.

Thank God. I knew it couldn't be this easy.

22

———

The entire world from the flowers to the fake sky shook. I let go of my hold on Baros, but he held on to me. His pale gaze raked over me with concern etched in his brows.

"Are you all right?" he asked.

"I'm not sure?"

Physically, I was fine. It was my insides that were messed up. My blood was warm. I felt it rushing to my cheeks like I was blushing or something. The valves of my heart must have come loose because the organ felt like it was tumbling around in my chest cavity. The corners of my eyes were stretching wider and wider like I was some virginal maiden come face-to-face with a knight in shining armor.

And that shining light was centered on Leonidas Baros.

I blinked rapidly to clear my vision. But my head was still muddled. Baros tucked me into his side as we surveyed our surroundings.

Well, he surveyed the field for new threats. I was too busy checking him out, trying to fathom what was happening between us.

He'd never coddled me. Not ever. He'd clean the mat with my ass and then demand I stand and take more. Even when we began knocking boots, he didn't shelter me from any threat. But he was holding my hand right now.

Then I noticed it. The hand that he held was my sword hand. Ah, so that was his game.

"Here," he said. And then he handed me his freaking sword.

He handed me his xiphos. A Spartan never relinquished his sword or shield. Their mothers told them to come home with it or on it.

My fingers tried to grip the hilt and failed. Before it clattered to the ground, I managed to get my palm securely around the leather bound handle. I brought it towards me like a mother would a newborn child.

Baros had never trusted me with this, his most prized possession, ever before. This was the seat of his power. The armor around his heart. And it was in my hands.

"I think we're meant to go deeper," he said.

My breath caught. My fingers tightened on the hilt, bringing it up to my heart. They were words I never expected to pass his lips, but now that I heard them, I finally admitted that they were the exact words I'd been waiting to hear for all my life.

"Loren?"

"Yes," I answered. "Yes," I nodded. "Yes." I took a step towards him.

He held out his hand. I reached for him. His brows screwed, and then he leaned in and retrieved his sword.

I looked down at my empty hands. The sound of steel against stone brought my gaze back up. I hadn't noticed until this second that we were standing before a cave. Baros had moved aside a boulder, which is why he'd handed me his sword. And now he was getting rid of some vines that blocked the entrance, which is why he'd taken his sword back from me.

Right. The ring. That's what he was here for. That was his goal.

I shook off the childish fantasy that had clouded my judgment and got back in the game. Two of

Gyges's eye cameras were staring at me. Mocking me, more like it.

What had the people seen in that moment when I'd been daydreaming? Had they seen the little girl whose head had been filled with fairytales? Well, she was gone. She'd hardly had the chance to live. I'd had to grow up quickly as the real world yanked those silly stories out of my reach. But I did remember another story. One that was far more useful.

"Plato said that Polemarchus had found the ring in a cave," I said.

Baros nodded. "If the stories in *The Republic* are true, then there will be a bronze horse with a dead man inside. He'll be wearing the ring."

"Do you think it'll be that simple? That we just walk inside and take the ring off a dead man."

"Let's go inside and see."

Baros reached for my hand again. Instead of placing my hand in his, I pretended I misunderstood the gesture. I took it to mean that he was allowing me to precede him inside, and I did exactly that. I couldn't let myself believe it meant anything else.

I went ahead of him, getting a head start. But I didn't exactly know what my end game was anymore? I should be trying to keep him from the ring, lead him on a wild goose chase until Geraint woke up, and then we could both overpower him. Right?

That had been my plan when I'd knocked Geraint out with my magical Vulcan death grip. If it worked. But if we overpowered Baros, Geraint would insist we take him back to the Olympians who would revoke his soul-contract with them.

On the other hand, I could let Baros get the ring. I could let him gain his freedom. Then the Greeks couldn't touch him. He'd be able to live out the rest of his days anyway he chose.

My traitorous heart dared to ask the question; what if he chose to spend those days with me like he'd whispered over the pillow last night? Was that what I wanted? For him to come with me to Camelot? Arthur would never stand for it.

So, what? Was I going to leave Camelot and my family for Baros? Even if I wanted to, and I'm not saying for certain that I did, I couldn't remain too long off a ley line.

All I could do right now was to put one foot in front of the other as we ventured deeper into the cave. Two of the camera eyes preceded us inside. Their light illuminated a tomb and the bronze statue of a horse that stood at the center of the cave.

What I didn't expect was for the man who was supposed to be inside the horse to be a giant. And he wasn't dead. He was wide awake.

The behemoth turned to us as we approached. A fire blazed beside him from a hearth dug into the wall of the cave. The giant held the ring in his hand. It lay in his open palm as though he were baiting us to try and take it.

Beside me, I felt the tension rolling off of Baros's shoulders as he eyed the ring, his freedom, his salvation. His hand tightened on his sword. His heels came up off the ground as though he were preparing to charge the giant.

"Who seeks the ring?" the giant asked. His voice boomed as though it came through loud surround-sound speakers.

"I do." Baros stepped in front of me. He didn't lower his sword, and his tense body remained ready to attack.

I felt a bit miffed that he didn't give me a chance to address the giant. I was a contender, too, after all. But that wasn't the plan, at least not the way Baros saw it. I was admittedly in between plans right now.

"What is your sacrifice?" asked the giant.

Baros turned back to me. His gaze lowered, and his chin dipped to his chest. My blood went hot again, and my poor, detached heart sank into my gut.

I should've known. I was the sacrifice. He was going to give me to the giant.

But instead of reaching for me with this free hand, Baros set his sword down. My blade was still snug in the satchel hanging over my shoulder, hiding out as a retractable cane. It would take but a second to reach for it and defend myself against ... a ring?

With his sword hand free, Baros yanked the ancient ring off his finger.

"This was my wife's ring," he said.

It took me a moment to understand. But when I did, my sword hand ached to be filled so that I could cut off his balls.

"Your wife," I growled. "Your wife, who's been dead for hundreds of years, is the most precious thing to you?"

"I'm letting her go so that we can be together."

Yeah, no. Somehow that didn't make it better. Had his wife endured slight after humiliation after rejection from him for a decade? Did his wife have to pretend that none of it affected her while still hoping for his attention?

No. Because she was dead. I was the live, warm

body that played second fiddle to a pile of bones. Hell, she probably wasn't even bones anymore. She was more likely dust. I was competing with dust, and I'd lost.

Baros approached the giant and handed him the ring. The giant took the ring and turned it over in his meaty palm. But then he shook his head.

"No," the giant said. "There is something more precious to you." The giant's gaze shifted to me.

Me? He was looking at me. I was more precious than Baros's wife.

I wanted to pump my fist into the air. I kicked at the dust on the floor of the cave even though I knew it wasn't anywhere near where Queen Gorgo was buried. But then, as the dust around my boot settled, reality hit me.

I was more precious than Baros's long-dead wife.

I reached into my satchel and grabbed my sword.

23

Rocks crunched under Baros's booted heels. They cracked and splintered, falling to pieces, turning to dust as he made his way to me. I didn't look up. I didn't want to see.

There might be pity stretched across his brow. There might be a deep V of resolve. There also was the slimmest chance that there might possibly be an arch of surprise that I would believe him capable of such a betrayal.

"Look at me, Lolo."

I closed my eyes. It was a stupid thing to do, to have my back turned and my eyes closed in the face of an adversary. But I was a stupid girl. I'd always been stupid when it came to this man. I'd missed so much out of life because I was stupid for him.

I'd never had a boyfriend, only a string of lovers that all paled when I inevitably compared them to him. I'd never been swept off my feet because he'd taught me to plant my feet in a wide fighting stance, giving my opponents my profile with my shoulder first and never my front where my heart was. I'd never heard those three little words, all because he told me they were fairytales for weaker women, and I was a fighter.

"Look at me, Lolo."

In the end, I did as I was told. I always did what he told me to do, hoping that he would one day see something special in me, something that would make him choose me and only me. There; I admitted it.

I was in love with Leonidas Baros. Had been for nearly my entire life. The moment I believed that he might finally feel the same way as I did, the earth literally opened up and shifted. All because I'd been stupid enough to dream, to hope it could be me, that I might be that girl who could get the fairytale.

Stupid.

I was stupid.

But I wasn't a coward.

I turned around, and I faced him. But I didn't raise my head. Instead, I raised my sword.

I saw his feet. He stood in a wide stance. He didn't even have the grace to give me his shoulder like a warrior would. It felt like a slight, and so I lifted my head. I was even more confused at what I saw.

Baros had his hands open, arms spread at his sides. His sword was sheathed. He took a step, approaching me slowly, like the wounded animal that I was.

"Put your sword down," he said.

I double fisted my blade.

"It's me, Loren."

"I know," I said. "That's why I've got a sword in front of my heart."

"You think I'm going to hurt you?"

I rocked back on my heels, but I didn't lower my blade. "You do it all the time. For as long as I've known you. You've broken my skin, my heart, my spirit. And I've let you because I thought I loved you. But this is not what love feels like. And the funny thing is, I know that. I know what love is like. It's not like I was a damaged girl with daddy issues. I was loved. I was just stupid for you. I'm not gonna be stupid anymore."

"Good," Baros said. "Then be smart and put down your sword. Don't make this hard."

"You want to cut out my heart with your blade so you can give it to a giant, and you want me to hold still?"

"Only because you mean the world to me."

A horrible sound rose from my chest, like a wounded animal being left in agony after a hunter's bullet or arrow missed a vital organ. Then the damned bastard just left it there to die instead of putting it out of its misery. It was cruel. And so I did what any animal on the brink of death would do to its attacker, I lashed out.

The next cry that left my lips was a guttural wail. My attack was sloppy. It was clumsy. But my wrathful strike was filled with the power of a decade of hurt. As always, Baros simply sidestepped my feelings.

I slashed at him. I slashed him for all the times I sat by the phone waiting for him to call. I slashed at him for every time I found another woman's number in his phone or saw lipstick on his shirt. I slashed and slashed, but I couldn't make the kill strike.

I wasn't done. I turned, swinging my blade in an arc. He leaned back, just an inch beyond my reach.

"It's true," he said, easily stepping out of my way as I continued to strike out at him. "You do mean a lot to me."

"If that were true, you wouldn't have stuck your nose up every skirt that came by."

I aimed for a low blow, but Baros hopped out of my reach so that I couldn't decapitate the little head that did most of his thinking.

"Is that what this is about?" he asked. "You know they didn't mean anything to me. Just warm bodies to feed my appetite. You were always my number one girl. Doesn't this prove it?"

He motioned to the giant sitting off to the side watching the fight with vague interest. I came to a standstill as I looked at the giant and the glistening ring sitting idly in his palm, waiting patiently for its new master.

"Doesn't this prove the depth of my feelings for you? That I care so much for you that I need to give you up?" Baros's face softened and his hand, still empty of a sword, reached out to me.

"Oh, my God, Lenny." I stared at his open palm. Tears pricked the corners of my eyes as my emotions overwhelmed me. "That is the douchiest thing that has ever been said to any woman in the history of the world. I'm totally calling *Cosmo*. You'll be a centerfold spread."

I couldn't believe I'd done it. I'd forgotten the cardinal rule. I'd pretended that the universal truth was a myth when it came to this man. But he was just like all the rest of them. He was a god-damned dud. There truly was no such thing as a fairytale. At least not for me.

"Love doesn't mean sacrifice," I shouted at the confused arch above his vacant gaze. "I mean it does, when you're hurting yourself. But not when you're hurting the other person in order to make yourself stronger. That's abuse."

Slowly his brow straightened. Then his open palm closed. And finally, his hand lowered. "Fine. Have it your way."

He unsheathed his blade. Then he sank his weight into a fighting stance. This time, he gave me his shoulder.

He didn't wait for me. He advanced. When the feel of his blade against mine rang so loud that my eardrums felt they would burst, I knew that he'd been holding back on me not only with his heart but with his sword. Like the ache that spread throughout my chest, I knew that this physical contest was another bout that I'd lose with his man. He was going to take it all from me.

And then it happened.

I'd managed to get free of his last attack. I'm pretty sure he'd allowed it. But I saw by the straight score of his brow, the pensive line of his lips, that he was done giving me anymore chances.

"*En guarde*, Lolo."

I took a deep breath, fully aware that it might be my last. Then I lunged into him. He held for a second until my blade was nearly upon him. Not until I extended myself, did he offer a defense.

Just like when I was seventeen, just like when we were in Eleusis, just like when we'd been in the arena, he parried. The flick of his wrist moved my blade aside. Baros's forte met my hilt, and I lost control of the fight.

His blade was at my neck. All he needed to do was flick his wrist one more time and riposte. He took a moment to gaze at me, as though taking a moment to remember my features.

My mind may have been playing tricks on me, but it looked as though there was a spark in his white eyes. My brain swore that that spark looked slightly—just a bit—like something that could've possibly been adoration.

"We all must sacrifice for the greater good, for the glory of Sparta," he said.

"I'm not a god-damned Spartan. I'm a knight and a Galahad girl."

Leonidas Baros, the man I loathed to admit that I

loved, stood over me. There was actual remorse on his face as he looked down. He leaned over me like he was going to kiss me before he slit my throat.

"Back away from her."

Baros's eyes narrowed. His brows rose in surprise as he recognized Geraint's voice. Then his jaw clenched, and his nostrils flared as he looked back down at me.

Seriously? He looked at me as though I was the betrayer?

"Stay out of this Geraint," I said.

"Can't," said Geraint, advancing on us with his sword raised. "I took an oath to come to the aid of all of my brothers."

The blade at my throat was suddenly an insignificant nuisance as I digested Geraint's words. I was spent emotionally. I had lost physically. But, wonder of wonders, I still had a moral leg to stand on. And so, while Baros spared Geraint a moment of his attention, I focused on the fire burning beside the giant and began a chant.

"Don't worry, sir," Baros was saying. "You'll have your turn as soon as I do away with this traitor."

"She's no traitor," said Geraint. "She was just on the wrong side having put her faith in the wrong people. She has her family now, people who will never lead her astray."

Baros scoffed and looked down at me. His mouth opened as though he were going to say something more, but he paused. His gaze focused on my moving lips. His ears twitched as though they were trying to hear what I was saying.

A wind kicked up in the room as the fire blazed brighter. The flames leaped outwards, blasting the room with light and heat. Baros's hold on me broke, and we all went clattering to the floor. All of us, except the giant, who glanced at the fire with the barest of interest.

A dark head poked out of the flames of the fire. Hades looked around, confusion in his eyes until he saw me. His brows rose in a question. Before I could answer, his gaze found Baros.

"Ah, Baros. There you are."

Baros's eyes widened impossibly large as the Greek God of the Underworld stepped out of the flames. Baros's eyes went to the giant's palm where the ring rested. Then he turned on me. "How could you?"

"What? Were you expecting a fairytale? A happily-ever-after after you slit my throat?" I said.

"Happiness is a constant, hard-fought battle to be won. You taught me that."

"Well said, Dame Galahad," said Hades. Then he reached out to Baros.

Before I had even a second to think about changing my mind, Baros was pulled into the fire. His protests extinguished by the flames as he was consumed.

There was a moment of deafening silence in the cave. And then cheers. The cave fell away, and we were back at the center of the arena. I heard the unmistakable voice of Gyges. Purple filled my vision as the sadistic fairy appeared before me. I was too distressed to hear a word he said.

Then there were arms around me, holding me tightly and shielding me from the accolades of consigning the man I loved to a death sentence. I turned my face into Geraint's chest and began to sob. He swept me off my feet, and I let him carry me away.

The ringing in my ear was a dull, somber tone. It matched the slow pulse of my heartbeat. The phone lay beside my head on speaker mode because my hands were to limp to grasp onto anything, even though I was trying to reach out to someone. But Nia's phone rang and rang and then went to voice mail. Like the last twenty times I'd called her.

I pushed up from my prone position in my bed. There was silence in this part of the castle as everyone was down in the dining hall. Well, almost everyone.

I couldn't hear them, but I could feel Morgan and Arthur arguing in the Great Hall. Well, Morgan was arguing. I felt the modulations of her emotions even though I couldn't hear her words. Arthur's punctuated silences and stillness were deafening, but he wasn't unaffected emotionally. I'd expected to feel anger as he glared at her, but instead, there was awe, and admiration, and something else I couldn't quite put my finger on.

Beyond those two, I could feel each of the townsfolk's energy signature, practically see their life force as they all arranged themselves at tables. I felt their joy, their love, and even some of their attentions as a few points of energy hailed me in acknowledgment. Someone, likely Igraine, gave me a tug, inviting me to join them. But I wasn't ready to face my family, not while I was still in mourning for what I'd lost.

I turned and looked out my bedroom window. The sun had set and the moon turned over another day. It had been three days since the tournament. The fae had cleared out moments after their fun was over. With their departure, and no one left holding the magical spell, the underground arena had fallen away.

I couldn't remember how we'd gotten out. Nor how we'd returned back home. I just remembered opening my eyes to the comforter that had belonged to my mother.

A knock sounded at the door. It wasn't the secret

knock that Gwin and Morgan and I had created. It was the knock of authority; the way a police officer would pound a doorframe before barging in.

Geraint.

When I didn't move fast enough, the knight opened the unlocked door. His eyes were closed as he waved a steamy bowl in front of his face. "Loren? You decent?"

A joke was on the tip of my lips, but my tongue felt too heavy to make it. "I'm dressed."

He opened his eyes and took me in. Then he winced.

I hadn't looked in a mirror for days, not since we got back. Somehow I had—or someone had—changed me out of the clothing I'd worn in the arena—probably Morgan. All my outer cuts and scrapes were healed—probably Gwin. But I was still ragged inside. If anyone looked in my eyes, they'd clearly see it.

Geraint looked into my eyes. He held up the bowl. It smelled awful, like offal. I took it from him and began shoveling the innards down my raw throat.

Geraint took a seat at the foot of my bed. He remained quiet while I ate, but that wasn't a very long time. "I heard from the Olympians," he said.

I didn't meet his gaze.

"Zeus has returned," he continued. "A date has been set. Do you want to know any more details?"

I shook my head.

"If you want to go to Athens, I'll come with you."

I looked up into his dark eyes. No, they weren't dark. They were hazel. It's just that there were many dark flecks in the hazel that made them appear darker than I'd originally thought. I'd never noticed.

"You'd do that?" I said.

"Of course," he said. "We're brothers."

I sniffled. Then I covered by punching him in the shoulder like a real brother would. "Thanks, but no. I already said my goodbyes."

Those goodbyes had been about the time when Baros had held a blade to my throat preparing to spill my life's essence to save his own. I might hate him, but I didn't want to see him die. If I had wanted to see it, I'd have done it myself.

Besides, I was weak. I'd always gone back to him in the past. And every time I did, I managed to trip and fall into him. He deserved what was coming to him.

I set the empty bowl aside and brought my knees to my chest. I expected Geraint to leave as melancholy settled over me, but he kept his seat.

"Gyges is gone," he said. "And so is the Ring of Invincibility, since no one claimed it that night."

I rubbed my nose against my knees and then rested my chin on my kneecaps as I looked at Geraint. There were dark spots under his eyes like he hadn't slept any of the three nights we'd been home. There were new wrinkles in his brow, as though something pressed on his mind.

"But now that he's on our radar," Geraint continued, "we'll be ready the next time he surfaces to play his sick games."

Geraint's lower lip curled in undeniable hatred. It caught me off guard and caused me to lift my head to see it better. This was nothing like the looks he'd given me when he protested my claim to the seat of Galahad. And I knew why. I was sure Geraint wanted to find Enid more than he wanted a crack at Gyges.

"Hey." I reached out my hand to him. "If she wants your help, she'll come to you."

Geraint stared at my palm, then he looked up into my eyes. "You think so?"

"I saw the way she looked at you when she had you all tied up with vines. Like she wanted to do more. Like she wished no one else was present so she could have her wicked way with you."

He shoved my open palm aside, but he did it

with a mocking smile. We shared a well-needed laugh for a moment. But all too soon, his face sobered.

"You good?" he asked.

Was I? I didn't know. But that's not what he meant. I shrugged one shoulder. "You?"

He shrugged one shoulder, too. Then he held out his palm to me. I grasped it immediately and held on. Neither of us said anything for a moment. We just sat there, holding on, taking strength from one another, but giving a piece of ourselves in return.

"I'll let you rest." He reached out and rubbed my shoulder. It was comforting this time. Like a big brother would give to his annoying little sister.

Geraint opened the door and headed out, but not before turning back and offering me another smile. It was a smile of solidarity; a smile that said he was here if I needed to talk. But there was also a wince at the corner of his eye that said he was a man and he'd rather not talk about his feelings. I laughed and shooed him out. I heard his sigh of relief as he shut the door.

When the door was firmly closed behind him, and I was sure no one else approached my room, I reached into my pocket and pulled out the Ring of Invincibility.

There had been a moment when Gyges had stood in front of me at the end of the tournament. He'd spoken to me, but I hadn't heard him. He'd taken my hand, and I hadn't pulled away from him. I'd been too busy trying to hold my tears at bay.

Later, when Geraint had placed me in my bed, and Morgan had changed my clothes, and Gwin had healed my wounds, I opened my clenched fists to find the ring. I knew I should take it to Arthur. And I would. Eventually.

The door to my bedroom creaked open again. Before Geraint poked his head back inside, I fisted the ring and shoved my hand beneath the covers.

"By the way," said Geraint. "Igraine said you should come down. She said a friend just landed and will be here soon."

My eyes widened. There was only one person I wanted to talk to. Nia.

"Thanks, I'll be down in a second."

Geraint nodded and closed the door again.

I looked at the ring for another couple of seconds. Then I slipped it on my finger. But I didn't disappear. I didn't feel any different. Not invincible, anyway. I still felt like a vulnerable little girl with a broken heart.

Was this yet another trick of Gyges? Was he

trying to see if I would turn the ring over or keep it to myself? I wouldn't be surprised.

It didn't matter. I wasn't going to do anything with the ring. I would turn it over to Arthur to put in the vault. Soon. But for now, I put the ring back in my pocket.

25

s I made my way down the hall, I took in the portraits of the knights who'd come before me. They were all men. They all stood or sat with their chests puffed proudly at the great honor that they'd each earned.

I took a deep breath as I came to stand before the portrait of the last Sir Galahad, my mother's father. This was a habit of mine. I'd been coming to stare at this portrait nearly every day since I'd been in residence in Tintagel, and still, I couldn't see the resemblance.

Sure, there was the golden hair, the blue eyes, the proud chin. But I wasn't sure if I favored him in any other way. It was said that Galahad was thought to be the most chivalrous of knights. That was quite a lot to live up to for a girl whose morals weren't still screwed on so tight.

Down the hall, I heard footsteps. I looked up to see Arthur coming out of the Throne Room. Over the past three days, I'd been neglecting my duties as a knight, but no one had chastised me.

I'd been through an ordeal. No one here had ever had to send someone they loved to the executioner. Well, no, Arthur had. But he'd shown mercy to his brother who was now in the infirmary. If anyone would understand what I'd been through with Baros, it would be Arthur.

I palmed the ring in my pocket, twiddling it between my thumb and forefinger. I should have turned it over to Arthur the first day I'd been home. It was what my grandfather would've done.

"We're headed out," Arthur said when he spotted me. "You wanna come? I'll be the first to buy you a stiff drink."

I smiled up at him, catching the ring in the palm of my hand. I fisted it and brought my hand out of my pocket.

"I'd gut that Baros if he wasn't already set for death," said Arthur.

I crossed my arms over my chest and, keeping my hand closed, I turned my heavy fist into my heart.

"You deserve better," Arthur said. "You know that."

I knew it. I believed it even. I just wasn't ready to accept it as my due. Not just yet.

"Thanks for the offer of a drink," I said unable to meet his gaze. "Can I have a raincheck? A storm check, actually, because when I do come out with you guys, I plan to get stupid drunk."

Arthur chuckled. It was a nice sound. I realized I hadn't heard it before. He'd always been so stern with me. But in his defense, I wasn't the easiest person to lead.

"Of course," said Arthur. "You're family. But, hey, don't wallow over that demon for too long."

"I won't. I'll come out next time. I'm expecting company tonight."

As if on cue, the doors to the castle opened, and a dark figure crossed the threshold.

"Loren, seriously?" growled Arthur. "He's no better than Baros."

Tresor Mohandis ignored Arthur's jab as he walked into the castle. He was dressed all in black, which complemented his sand-kissed skin. His broad shoulders were backlit by the moonlight, making him look like an ethereal god, not a man. He was hot enough to take my mind off of Baros for a second, but only a second. Because then I looked up at his face.

That handsome face that I would always sneak glances at when he was looking at Nia was drawn and somber. He had the same dark shadows beneath his eyes and the same heavy crease to his brow as Geraint. What kind of ordeal had he just come through?

I looked past him, but there was no one behind him. I opened my mouth to speak, but it filled with such dread that I had to close it, swallow, and try again.

"Where's Nia?" But my voice was a whisper against Tres's heavy boot falls.

I couldn't remember the names of the people who'd come to tell me that my dad was dead. I couldn't remember if it had been two or three people. I couldn't remember their heritage or the colors of their eyes. All I could remember was that grim expression. The same expression that Tres wore now as he came to stand before me.

I stepped back from him. Then I took a few steps away as he kept coming toward me. I wanted to run. But I didn't. I stood and faced him and his haunted eyes.

It was absurd. Nia couldn't die. She was immortal.

I pulled my hand out of my pocket. In it was my phone. I flipped it open and dialed Nia's number.

Just like the twenty-odd times it had done before, it rang and rang again. It went on like that for a quarter of an hour before I'd even look up at Tres to listen to him. And still, I couldn't believe him. The only thing that I could think was that Nia would tell me if she was dead. It was stupid, I know, but it was all that made sense.

Suddenly, the earth was coming out from under me. The walls around me were moving. Then I felt something under my butt and something cold in my hands. It was the stiff drink that Arthur had promised. He was pushing it into my hands.

I drank from the cup, downed it, and then motioned for another. And then another. I was tipsy before I gained the presence of mind to finally listen to Tres's words.

He told me about the Balam and Mohegan

shifters, about the God Twins, and the Serpent Mound. About an underground cave and a door of light. Nia and Zane had fallen through a crack in the earth, fallen to their deaths.

The last time Nia had been here, Igraine had told her of a prophecy. I knew about the prophecy, but Nia hadn't told me the particulars. She'd insisted on leaving me behind while I was still recuperating from my run in with the Spear of Destiny. She'd promised that she'd return. She'd lied.

But Nia wouldn't do that. Not to me. She would tell me if she were going to die.

It was the same argument I'd had with the bearers of bad news about my father. He'd always told me where he was going and when he'd be back. He'd always checked in when he was away too long.

Nia was my bestfriend. She would've told me. And so my mind refused to believe it.

"We need to go down there," I said.

"Loren ..." Tres's voice was so soft.

He'd only ever growled at me. I didn't know he was capable of such gentleness. It caught me off guard, but only for a second. This was Nia we were talking about.

"We have to save her," I said. "There has to be some way into the garden."

"She's gone, Loren," said Tres. "They're both gone."

His brown eyes were filled with such sorrow and guilt. Tres loved Nia. I knew he cared for Zane too, even though the two of them had been at war over the same woman. For the briefest of seconds, I felt an intense moment of jealousy. For just once in my life, I wished a man would have that depth of feeling for me.

"Who are you looking for, dear?"

We all turned to see Igraine. I looked around, finally noticing where we were. In the kitchens. I supposed Arthur or Tres, I wasn't sure who, had carried me in here.

On the table, was the same bottle of rum I'd used to make Midnight Margaritas with Gwin and Morgan just a week ago. Those spirits had given me such joy then. They were doing a terrible job of trying to cover my pain now.

"Nia," I said to Igraine. "We're looking for Nia. Tres says she's dead. But she's not. She can't be. Is she?"

"Oh," said Igraine, her eyes going fuzzy like they did when she was having one of her visions. She reached out for something to steady herself. Arthur was there by her side in an instant. "She's not dead."

I turned to glare at Tres, ready to say I told you so.

"But I saw them," he said. "I saw them fall. They couldn't have survived."

"They didn't," said Igraine.

"What?" I shouted. I ran to Igraine. "But you said she's not dead."

Igraine blinked her eyes, trying to focus. The old witch had no control over her powers, but I could see her wrangling for control. Nia had been coming to visit her for centuries. She loved her as much as I did.

"I see her," Igraine said. "She didn't survive, but she's not dead."

I stopped trying to make any of it make sense. I just needed the facts. "Igraine, please, tell me where Nia is."

"She's with her parents in the garden. But she can't leave. I think she's grounded."

"How do we get there? How do we get to the garden?"

"The only way into Eden's garden," said Igraine, "is with the Hammer of God."

Join Loren and Tres as they search for a way to save Nia and Zane in
The Hammer of God,
Book Three in the Misadventures of Loren.

9 781954 181366